STOCKPORT
METROPOLITAN BOROUGH COUNCIL

Libraries,
Advice and
Information

CMU
10\18

HET 11\19

meth

Please return/renew this item by the last date
shown.
Books may also be renewed by phone or the
Internet

TEL: 0161 217 6009
www.stockport.gov.uk/libraries

D1439808

Other novels by Chris Simms:

Psychological thrillers
Outside the White Lines
Pecking Order

Supernatural thrillers
Sing Me To Sleep

DI Spicer series
Killing the Beasts
Shifting Skin
Savage Moon
Hell's Fire
The Edge
Cut Adrift
Sleeping Dogs

DC Iona Khan series
Scratch Deeper
A Price To Pay

Previously published as *Rats' Nest*

To Mum, for making me wear that 'beard' at the school fete…

CHAPTER 1

Something about the man made Father Ian Thompson uneasy. The elderly priest glanced again towards the front pews, seeking out the lone silhouette. The person had been sitting there for over an hour. In all that time, he had moved only twice. First was when the front door banged shut as the last choir members left. Second was when the cleaner, Mrs Reynolds, dropped a can of polish. The fact unexpected noises caused the man to flinch didn't trouble the priest. What did disturb him was where the man cast his anxious glances. Rather than looking to his sides, he had tipped his head back, searching the dimly-lit rafters and shadowy ledges high above.

After attaching a couple of notices to the board at the entrance, the priest smoothed a stray lick of white hair back in place and made his way slowly down the central aisle. The squeak of his shoes on the wooden floor caused the man's head to twist momentarily. He then looked up briefly before returning his stare to the altar.

The priest gave a gentle cough as he reached the end of the aisle. 'I don't wish to disturb your thoughts, but the church is closing now.'

The man's gaze shifted to the effigy of Christ mounted high up on the wall beside the altar. Late afternoon sunlight was blazing through a stained glass window, bathing the crucified figure in fiery blotches.

Father Thompson examined the man's profile as he

waited for a reply. The oily black strands which lay across the crown of his head failed to hide the pink scalp beneath. Stubble coated his cheeks and his tie had been yanked loose from his collar. The priest caught the fruity smell of alcohol. Beside the man was a black leather attaché case. 'Of course,' the priest added, 'if you need a few more – '

'Do you believe in ghosts?' The man's voice was low and raw.

He had a despair about him; the kind the priest was more used to seeing at funerals. Relatives, forced into sudden confrontation with mortality and all that it entailed. 'Ghosts? That's a tricky question to answer.'

The man's throat moved as he swallowed. His head turned in the priest's direction, eyes roving hungrily. 'But you believe something lives on once the body is dead? The essence of a person?'

The priest noticed the lower rims of the man's eyes were bright red. 'I do.'

'Then can I...I'd like to describe something to you, then.' He raised a hand and massaged one temple with small, agitated movements. A dark strand slipped across his knuckles and he raked it back. 'Can I?'

The priest frowned, curious but now slightly apprehensive. 'Of course.'

The man immediately reached for his attaché case. The only sound was the clinks of its twin buckles being hastily undone. 'Do you think...might a ghost have the power to harm the living? Could it want to do damage? Be motivated by revenge or retribution: things like that?'

The priest paused. Like cloud shadow across the sea, an ominous feeling passed over him. 'Those are unusual – and serious – questions. Why do you ask?'

He got the bag open. 'I think I've made a mistake. A terrible, terrible mistake.'

CHAPTER 2

The priest eased himself onto the pew and placed his hands across his paunch. He suspected he wouldn't make it to Iceland before it shut. He pictured the freezer compartment stacked with the one person meals. He'd planned on having a Shepherd's Pie, followed by apple tart and custard. As he sat back, he sensed that being beside the man might suit the coming conversation; eye contact would only be possible if both men sought it. 'What kind of a mistake do you think you've made?'

The man sniffed. 'My life.'

The priest turned his head a fraction. A desolate smile was stretching the man's lips. 'Go on.'

'I work for a magazine.'

The priest had to shuffle a little closer to make out the whispered words. 'A magazine?'

'You may have heard of it. It's called *Snapped!*'

The priest nodded, his stirrings of trepidation now replaced by something closer to disdain. He could picture the magazine's office; it featured often enough on the news. A journalist standing outside, describing the latest person attempting to sue the publication for libel. It was an ugly, modern block of a building, all harsh angles and reflective black glass. Monolithic. It reminded the priest of a monstrous four wheel drive with mirror windows: the people inside could observe the world while remaining unseen.

The magazine itself was usually placed high on newsagents' shelves. It consisted of scandalous reports about famous people, conjecture on their love lives, mental health, or both. But what each story was based upon were photographs: the more lurid and intrusive, the better. It was pure celebrity tittle-tattle and – in the priest's opinion – a symptom of where society had gone so badly wrong. He knew the weekly magazine sold in its thousands. He gathered its online version was even more successful.

The visitor tapped a finger on the attaché case's leather handle. 'There are two different stories in the current issue. We ran them separately, but now,' he took a shallow breath in, 'now I think there's a connection. The stories are about the deaths of two women.'

The priest turned his head once more. The man had closed his eyes tight; the skin around them was pinched inward. The priest chose to say nothing and several seconds slid by.

Then the man shook his head, as if trying to rid it of an unwelcome thought. His eyes re-opened and he announced a name. 'Mandy Cost.'

The priest felt his face blanche. Glad the visitor was still staring straight ahead, he also turned to the altar, trying to gather his thoughts. Mandy Cost had been a regular visitor to the church. Though not a Catholic, she'd pop in for a confession of sorts. Sometimes for advice or guidance. Often just to air her doubts and fears in a place where she felt safe. A place free from the cruel flash of photographers' cameras. Then, around two months ago, she'd simply stopped coming. The lack of explanation had been tormenting the priest ever since. Was the man a reporter? If he was, how much did he know about what had developed between the two of them? 'Her name is vaguely familiar.'

'She used to come in here a bit, apparently. I'm not sure if you ever talked to her. You probably didn't even know who she was. Mandy was an ex-glamour model.

Then a singer, then a chat-show guest. Girlfriend – though always short-lived – to footballers, soap actors or businessmen.' The man shrugged. 'Someone who – in my line of work – we rely on to fill our pages. Last Saturday, she jumped through the second floor window of a beauty salon in Mayfair.'

The priest was well aware of Mandy's tragic end. The news reports had stunned him. Her lipstick may have been far too bright and her tops far too low – but he'd come to realise her sexualised exterior was just a shell. A shell that concealed a sensitive and thoughtful, if slightly confused, woman. He breathed out slowly through his nose. A sound of sympathy and regret: something to prompt the man to continue.

The visitor began reaching into the case. His fingertips trembled as if the dark interior concealed a trap. 'The coroner has yet to give a verdict. There's speculation she reacted badly to the local anaesthetic the salon had used; injections for her lips or face.' He drew his hand back and looked at the priest. 'I should have said. I'm a picture editor at *Snapped!* It's my job to direct photographers to jobs, select the images we'll use, negotiate a price from freelancers – that sort of thing. It's...it's not something I ever...I wanted to be a wildlife photographer, actually.' He raised his eyebrows. We all had dreams, the expression said. Before reality came crashing in. 'Anyway, I purchased a series of shots. Taken by a toggy who was – '

'Sorry: toggy. What's that?'

'Toggy? Right. A photo-journalist. Freelance. He comes to us with a lot of pictures, sometimes stories, too. So, he's outside the salon with his camera waiting for Mandy to emerge.'

And this, the priest thought, is why you're here. Guilt that you contributed to her death. Well, you'll have to work hard if you want forgiveness from me. Several times, Mandy had tottered through the church doors in tears, distraught at repeated violations of her privacy. 'His camera? Is not the correct term for people like him, paparazzi?'

The man weighed the comment up. 'He certainly does a bit of that, too. But Mandy worked with him. She'd tip him off about opportunities for – '

'Pardon?' the priest interrupted. 'She'd asked him to be there?'

'Precisely. It was part of the arrangement they had.'

The priest looked away. Mandy had never mentioned that she cooperated with any of the people who seemed to upset her so much. The worry that she may have said something returned.

'He was there to catch her as she came back out with her new short-haired look. Those long, silvery hair extensions of hers she had fitted a fortnight ago? She'd gone to have them taken out.'

'Really? Removed?' Even if he'd wanted to, the priest couldn't have missed the recent media coverage of Mandy, her ethereal mane stretching down her back. She'd looked magnificent. 'Hadn't that particular style really caught the public's attention?'

The man nodded.

'Why would she want to change it?'

'It's tied in with what's been happening.'

'Very well. Carry on.'

'So, this person was waiting on the far side of the street, fiddling with his viewfinder. He had just started taking a few test shots when there was movement up on the second-floor. At that precise moment, she came through the glass. He got the whole thing.' He bowed his head. 'We only used the photos of her on the pavement, once paramedics had covered her with a blanket. And one of the broken window frame she jumped through. But there were plenty of other images. Ones we didn't use out of respect.'

'Respect or decency laws?' The priest's voice was flat.

Something clattered and the man almost jumped to his

feet, panicked eyes sweeping about above them. Repelled as he was by the man, the priest placed a hand on his shoulder before gently calling out, 'Mrs Reynolds?'

His words hung in the still air. An elderly lady came into view, her stooped body almost enveloped by the gathering gloom. She was wheeling an unplugged vacuum cleaner. Above her, the patch of sunlight illuminating Christ had slid fractionally to the side. The fingertips of his outstretched left hand were now in shadow.

'Bless her. She recently lost her husband,' the priest said very quietly from the corner of his mouth. 'Keeping the church clean is something she volunteered to do.' He raised his voice, 'You needn't worry with that, Mrs Reynolds. Why not get off home?'

Her voice wavered thinly. 'Someone needs to give it a once over.' The vacuum was brought to a halt on the carpet before the altar.

'I'll do it then. I really don't mind. You've been working far too long as it is.'

The acknowledgement of her efforts caused a smile. Suddenly, she could have been fifteen. An infatuated school girl. 'That's nonsense. You have enough to be worrying about. It's the least I can do.'

The priest raised a palm. 'No, no. You've done plenty. Anyway, I think the thing needs replacing.'

She cocked her head. 'Why's that?'

He breathed out near silent words. 'That's torn it.' He lifted his voice again. 'It's not picking anything up. Honestly, though, you needn't – '

But the old lady was already patting the pockets of her apron. 'Where are my reading glasses? In my handbag, I think. Where did I put it?'

'One moment,' the priest said to the visitor, getting stiffly to his feet. 'I'll get them, Mrs Reynolds.'

As the priest headed off towards the far end of the church, the man sat back, gaze going to the thick locks that lay across Christ's shoulders. The old woman entered the periphery of his vision. She was coming over.

On reaching the end of the pew, she fixed him with a cold look. 'I'd ask you not to take advantage of Father Thompson's good nature,' she whispered.

The man stared back in surprise.

'I could smell the drink on you when you came wandering in. He doesn't need you robbing him of his valuable time. If you only knew how much –' A door closed and she glanced briefly back towards the altar. 'Just don't keep him here all evening. It's not fair on the poor man.'

She was back by the vacuum when Father Thompson reappeared. 'Here you are, Rosemary.'

She took the handbag with a thank you and he returned to where the visitor was sitting. 'Sorry, you were saying?'

The man floated a look in Mrs Reynold's direction then cleared his throat. 'The other story I wanted to mention was the murder of Maggy Wallace.'

The priest felt his eyebrows lift. The woman who lived up in Scotland? Surely not. What could possibly link her to Mandy Cost? 'You mean the lady who lived out in the woods? Who was murdered…I don't know, not that long ago…'

'Twenty days, to be exact.'

The priest slid his fingers together. Now this was odd. He was familiar with the sad sequence of events. Maggy Wallace had been a reclusive woman in her late fifties. She'd lived close to a village called Kilree, not far from Glasgow. The case had made the news because of its baffling nature. Her body had been found in her wooden cabin. Someone had throttled her – but the police couldn't work out why. Nothing appeared to have been taken from the cabin and a sexual motive had been quickly ruled out.

Much of the subsequent media attention had appalled the priest. Maggy Wallace may well have lived alone. She may well have been difficult to get on with: sharp-tongued on her occasional visits to the village and hostile to anyone she encountered in the woodland surrounding her home. But that didn't make her a witch. Claims like that belonged in a previous century – not within the pages of modern newspapers. He dreaded to think how *Snapped!* had portrayed the woman. 'Have they found who did it yet?'

'Gregory Lang, twenty-five, from Glasgow. He turned up at his local police station in a very distressed state, I gather. Could hardly sign the custody forms.'

The priest glanced at the man's profile. The information sounded first-hand. 'You read this in a paper?'

'No. The custody sergeant at the station told that toggy I mentioned.' He rubbed briskly at both cheeks with the heels of his hands and blinked a few times. 'A lot of what I'm about to say has yet to make the news. If it ever will. The toggy? He also got to speak directly with Gregory Lang.' He licked his lips, eyes swivelling in the priest's direction.

The fear that filled them made the older man want to look away. 'How did he manage that?'

'You'd be surprised at what's possible. Call it tricks of the trade.'

Once again, the priest felt uneasy. Warily, he asked, 'You've been speaking to this toggy person?'

'I have. And this is what Gregory Lang told him.'

CHRIS SIMMS

CHAPTER 3

'You're dumping me?' Greg Lang stared into his pint glass. A torrent of bubbles swarmed up at him. He tracked some to the surface, where they simply vanished. 'That's it? We're done?'

The woman on the opposite side of the small table hesitated. She wondered whether to reach across and stroke his hand. But there was now a tension in his shoulders. Her hand stayed where it was; he'd been violent before, though not for several years. 'Greg, let's be honest here. We've been done a long time.'

He lifted his eyes. They shone wetly. 'Since fucking when?'

She wanted to avoid specifics. Pointing out examples of his many failings wasn't going to help. 'It's felt flat for...I don't know...a long while. You've known it, too. You have.'

He was absolutely still. Worryingly so. Cautiously, she continued. 'I mean, how often has it just been the two of us? Alone, chatting, cuddling. I can't remember.'

He raised his glass too quickly. The rim clicked against his teeth, a sharp, brittle sound. A couple of drips fell from his chin as he took a long gulp, then another. Peels of laughter broke from the group at the adjacent table. Two couples cracking up over something, a cluster of cocktails before them. His eyebrows dipped. 'You're seeing someone else. Who is he?'

She'd guessed this was coming. 'Greg, there's no other man.'

His eyes stayed locked on hers. 'Michelle, you think I'm a total fuckwit or something?'

Calmly, she held his gaze. 'Really, there isn't.'

He scrutinised her for a long moment. 'It's this business, then. That's the problem. Frigging Sheila, the bitch.'

She was careful to not show how much his comment hurt her. 'You can't blame this on Sheila.'

'Why the fuck not? It's her money.'

Sheila had been at beauty college with her. Her mum had died the previous year and Sheila got the house. She'd sold it and got in touch with Michelle. A hair and beauty salon: Michelle's knowledge of various beauty treatments, Sheila's hairdressing skills – and all her clients, once she judged the time was right to leave Toni & Guy's in the city centre.

Michelle sat back. This was an area she had no hesitancy defending. 'I've worked bloody hard to set this up. Hours.'

'I noticed.' His lips curled, but it wasn't a smile. He drank again. 'All the forms. Emails. Every minute at your computer.' He looked at her with defiance. 'If we're looking for reasons why.'

She wanted to cross her arms. 'And did you ever offer to help me? It could have been the two of us. We could have done it together. You weren't bothered.'

'With a hairdresser's? Me? Sweeping up and making old biddies brews. Fuck off.'

'I don't mean that – and you know it. Painting the place, getting the chairs bolted to the floor, putting mirrors up. Maybe doing more in the flat? I still cooked for you – even when I was too tired to eat anything myself.' She saw the comment had got through: his jaw had tightened.

'I'll not be anyone's maid. Or servant.'

This, she knew, was the real reason he'd done nothing.

Starting up the salon had upset the balance of their relationship. Worse, it had resulted in power for her. Power, money and purpose. 'I want to make something of my life – I got the chance and I have. Or at least, I am. Not sitting around, smoking the weed, selling pills, doing the same old stuff.'

He swung his head one way, then the other. Eyes taking in the bar's decor. Leather seats. Soft glows from hidden lights. Muted colours. Laughter again from the table nearby. One of the men reached across to the shoulder of the girl beside him. He started to remove a single hair from her collar. It was long, and he had to draw his hand back, like a magician producing something impossible. He let the golden strand hang for a second then parted his finger and thumb. Greg watched the affectionate gesture with a scowl on his face. 'So, this place counts for exciting? This makes the cut?'

He'd spat the last word out and she cursed her mistake. Of course a bar like this was going to rile him. She should have picked somewhere more basic – but the only place she knew like that was their old local. She'd spent too long in that shit heap. 'Listen, you'll see this makes sense. You will. Rent on the flat's paid until the end of the month. After that, it's up to you what you do with it.'

'What I want to do with it? Where'll you be?'

'I'll kip in the rooms above the salon.'

He stayed quiet for a second or two. 'You're moving out?'

'I need to get my head straight, Greg. We open for business next week – there's still so much to do. There's a wee kitchen and bathroom there. It'll do me for now.'

Things were moving too fast for him, she could see that. But it had to be like this. A clean break. Like how her dad used to despatch rabbits. Kinder that way.

He sucked back more lager, thinking. His eyes narrowed. 'You're going there tonight, aren't you? You've fucking planned all this out.' A few sets of clothes. Shoes.

Toiletries. He had no idea what items of hers were even left in their room. For all he knew, she'd sneaked most of it out. Her gym stuff, make-up, coats: he never checked her drawers or hanging space. Why would he? It was her who kept the flat tidy. 'What else is there already? A bed, I bet.'

Everything I need, she thought. And there's no bloody way you can get in, short of breaking down the door. 'A few bits and bobs. Greg, you don't want me in the flat. We'd both be sat there simmering, saying nothing. This way, we've got room to breathe.'

One of the women let out a sigh of amusement and he winced at the noise. The man next to her was shrugging a shoulder in response when he caught Greg's eyes. Held it for a nanosecond too long. Greg's glass banged down on the table. The man's glance dropped.

'What's the fucking joke over there?'

The nearest woman began to look over her shoulder, but the man said something under his breath, eyes fixed on his drink. She turned back.

'Greg, don't.' Michelle put a hand on his forearm. 'Let's move – '

He shook it off. 'No. I want to hear what this table of grinning twats is finding so funny. I want in on the joke.'

The group was now silent, heads bent, faces not moving. 'It was nothing, mate,' one of the men announced quietly. His accent wasn't from Glasgow. It was hardly even Scottish. Conversations were petering out all around them as the atmosphere thickened.

'Greg, I want to go – '

His head jerked like a poorly controlled puppet. 'Fuck off, you do. You fit right in. Come on, join the fuckers.' He stepped round the table, grabbed her chair and tipped it to the side.

She half-stumbled to her feet. 'Greg, please.'

'There you go.' He shoved the empty chair alongside the woman's. 'Shift across, Michelle here is joining you.

She's an uppity cow like you. Swop fucking business cards. She'll do your nails, maybe. Those poncey hot stones – she does them, too.' He leaned toward the woman's boyfriend. 'Ask her nicely, you might get a massage out of her, mate. Few more cocktails and you can all fuck each other.'

Three doormen were making their way across. Greg yanked his coat from the back of his chair. 'See you round, 'Chelle.'

Her arms were tightly clasped, face bright red. 'Come on, Greg, please – '

'Please? Please what?' he snarled. 'Please let you walk out on me with no bother?' he lifted a hand towards the security staff. 'I'm off, don't worry. A second longer in here and I'll be spewing down the walls.'

CHAPTER 4

He checked the phone's screen again. The message was still there; it wasn't a joke. On opening the message envelope, he'd half-expected the letters to start fading away, pixel-by-pixel. But they hadn't.

Hi Greg, you OK? Can we meet? Have some work you may like. Will pay you cash. Michelle X.

He studied the X. What sort of a kiss was it? A proper kiss? Or just one of those cheek-touch things he saw people do. Could it be that she was coming to her senses? That what she'd done to them had finally dawned on her?

He looked round the sparsely-furnished front room. It was now a few days since she'd turned up. Partick Thistle had been playing at home, so she knew he'd be out. Loads of stuff had gone. Once he'd calmed down, he walked round the flat, trying to work out what was missing.

Kettle. Bread maker. Toastie maker. Coffee maker. Set of sharp knives. Set of cutting boards. Juicer. Wall clock. Digital radio. Large wall mirror. Flat screen TV. Ikea chairs. CD player and docking station. Digital bathroom scales. Bedroom television. Bed side lamp. Digital alarm clock.

The only decent bit of electrical equipment she'd left was the Playstation, which was lucky: he'd bought that.

She'd tidied up a bit, too. Gathered up all the stuff from when she'd been researching the salon. Put it all in a box, only to leave it in the far corner. He hadn't chucked it out, even though the sight of it pissed him off. He retrieved the note she'd left on the windowsill. No kiss on that one. He read it again.

Popped by, but you weren't here. Grabbed the last of my things. Not sure if you're staying on. Will leave my set of keys with the landlord if you want them.

He couldn't dowse the feeling inside his stomach. Why clear out all her things then, a few days later, text him like this? Could she be trying to get back with him? Or at least sound things out? His shoulders drooped. Be serious. He thought about her little salon, Mishi's. Michelle and Shirley's, merged and shortened. He'd walked past it a couple of times. Only when it was dark – when those inside couldn't see out. She'd been in there, working away under the bright lights. Her appearance had made his throat tighten. She'd seemed happy. There was a bounce in her movements. Confidence. Energy. Less than two weeks away from him and she was a different person. He'd wanted to burst in and sweep the bottles from the shelves. He'd wanted to wrench the sinks off the walls. He'd wanted to pin her against the wall and kiss her so hard she couldn't breathe.

There was no sign of her through the plate glass window. A teenager with an immaculate blonde bob was in there: work experience or something, he concluded. Cheap labour. She was advancing towards the far wall, pushing a broom before her. When he opened the door, it set off a chime and she looked back, dismay on her face. 'We're finished for the –'

'Michelle in?'

She straightened up, eyes going to the doorway leading to the rear of the property. A voice – Michelle's voice – called out from within. 'Greg? Two ticks. Andrea, make him a tea, would you?'

Greg was wondering what she was up to back there as Andrea gestured to the seats beside him. 'Sit down. How do you take it?'

He plonked himself in the corner. 'White, two sugars, ta.' On the low table before him, a selection of magazines had been arranged in a fan shape. The stuff at the centre was up its own arse: *Vogue*, *Cosmopolitan* and *Glamour*. Off to the side tackier crap: *Look*, *Shout* and *Snapped!* Hairdressing ones were at the other end. Fifty quid's worth, easily. He checked the soft chair he was sitting on. Brand new. Three others to either side. The bouquet of flowers on the counter by the till didn't look cheap, either. She was blowing the bank loan he knew she'd taken out, that was for sure.

He crossed his legs and leaned back, not liking the fact he was being made to wait. Was she fucking him around? The young lass came back and he got a sneaky-peek down her top as she put the cup on the table. Black bra, lacy edge. She'd be worth a dig. 'Cheers.' He sought eye contact as she straightened up.

'A pleasure.' Her eyes touched his as she turned away.

He thought he detected a glimmer of interest. She probably lived in the city. Nice. He could picture a night in her flat, rutting away. She'd taken up the broom once more. It angled this way and that as she herded a thin ridge of hair snippings towards a larger pile in the corner.

'Greg, how are you doing? Thanks so much for coming.'

She was already through the doorway, walking towards him, eyes on his face. Business-like. Self-assured. For a horrible moment he thought she was going to offer to shake hands. Her arm was slightly raised, but then it dropped and she took the seat one away from him. She slid a magazine out from under her arm and placed it on the table. A copy of *Hello*. Some tosser couple with teeth whiter than toilets beamed up at him. He wanted to gob in their faces.

'What do you think?' Her manicured nails gave a little circle. 'Like it?'

Her manner threw him. She was expecting him to approve of the place? The very thing that had split them up? Her pet project. Her bridge to what she'd decided would be a better life – without him. 'Not bad.'

'Not bad.' She rolled her eyes. 'You never were one for sweet talk.'

Now she was speaking about him in the past. But with warmth and affection. He was confused. 'So, what's this thing you mentioned?'

She draped a hand across one knee. Her nail varnish was a shade of purple he'd never noticed before. Probably new. It matched the face of the watch she was wearing. That was definitely new.

'OK, so we do a range of stuff here. Hair in this area, beauty treatments in the rooms back there.' She nodded towards the doorway she'd come through. 'Since opening, I've had loads of calls. Mainly from companies trying to flog me stuff. Most of them I ignore. But I got one the other day that was a bit different. Do you know about hair extensions?'

He nodded at the cover of *Hello* magazine. 'Like that?' The woman on the front had thick tresses of black hair tumbling over one shoulder.

'Exactly,' Michelle smiled. 'That's definitely not hers. You know how it works?'

He shook his head.

'If you want hair like hers – but yours isn't that long – you get someone to weave a load of hair in. All sorts of singers and actresses have it done.'

A plastic clatter. Over in the corner, Andrea was now sweeping the cuttings into a dustpan. Her nose was wrinkled as she tipped them into a bin.

'The extensions need to be long,' Michelle continued. 'The longer, the better. And it has to be human. Synthetic stuff is...well, you can't style it the same. It sits differently, moves differently. Crap, basically.'

He kept his mouth closed and ran his tongue across the back of his teeth. Keep going, he thought.

'Now this big salon down in London has contacted me. Hair-extensions are what they specialise in. Dark hair's no problem to get hold of: tons of it's available from places like India and China. Blonde? Nowhere near as easy.'

'They don't just bleach the stuff?'

She shook her head. 'For a start, bleaching hair damages it, leaves it fragile. And dark hair is thicker, more coarse, than blonde. So even if you use bleach or dye, it still doesn't match the finer texture of Western hair.'

He looked about for an ashtray then decided it wasn't the sort of place where you could light up.

'This place in London,' Michelle continued, 'relies on a broker based in Kiev. The best possible hair – the gold standard – is something called Russian Virgin.'

'Oh yeah?' Greg smirked. 'How old?'

She managed a brief smile. 'Virgin means it's never been dyed, bleached, permed or straightened. Hundred percent natural. Hair like that is the softest, silkiest, best quality there is. It's also the hardest to find; it tends to come from rural communities where they eat a healthy, simple diet. No sugar, salt, alcohol, processed crap – it all affects the quality of the hair. This salon's problem is their broker just got arrested. He won't be coming back for a long time, apparently. They badly need fair hair. Not just blonde: unusual shades. Platinum, strawberry-blonde, copper, titian. They'll pay good money, too. The longer it is, the higher the price.'

He crossed his arms. 'What sort of money?'

She lifted an eyebrow. 'Four hundred quid for twenty-four inches' worth. Another ten quid for every inch after that. Andrea? Tell Greg what you made last week.'

Andrea sent a grin across to him. 'Eight hundred pounds.'

'You fucking what?' Greg spluttered. 'Was it down to

your ankles?'

Andrea laughed. 'To here.' She pressed a forefinger at a point just above her elbow.

'But she also found five other girls at her college with hair of a similar length,' Michelle said. 'We paid them a flat price – me and Andrea – and split the difference.'

Greg sat back. 'Who do I know with long hair? No one.'

'Doesn't matter. Around where you grew up. It's, you know – '

'Poor as fuck, yeah.'

'I'm thinking, you with your good looks...'

He shot her a glance, not sure if she was taking the piss.

'What? I'm serious. Look at you: half male-model, half boxer. Younger women, they love a bad boy. So, I'm thinking I give you a load of business cards. Nice ones with your name on. You scoot around handing them out to girls with long blonde hair. They come here, I pay them cash and they get a decent cut, like Andrea's. What do you reckon?'

'What would I be, your employee?'

'No. You'd be...I don't know. An agent? Yeah, an agent.'

'Like I work for myself? I decide the hours?'

'Absolutely. You'd be your own boss.'

'And what do I get?'

'A fifty-fifty split – same as Andrea got.'

He weighed things up. There were estates he knew of where people were desperate, proper desperate. Half the shops boarded up, folks wandering the streets with nothing in their pockets. Queues at the food banks. This could be good. And it meant contact with Michelle again. It was a pity he couldn't remove the hair himself. He imagined walking into the salon with an armful of...what...manes? Laying them down on the counter like a fur trapper at a trading post. 'How do I know you'll actually pay me for every lass I send through the doors?'

'You can do all your own bookings, see the accounts as well, if you want. There'd need to be some trust between us, though.'

Trust. The word hinted at a relationship. Working together. He pictured the two of them dividing up the cash, heading out for drinks together. It would be somewhere flash, too. He wouldn't mind. He held a hand out, happy now for a chance to shake.

CHAPTER 5

The bus laboured slowly on, leaving him with a face full of acrid fumes. He surveyed the empty street. Jesus, the place had got even more grim. Pebble-dash walls, unlit windows, sideways smoke leaking from a couple of chimneys.

The wind was just like he remembered. Steady and cruel. He regarded the nearby hills and could almost see the chill air flowing down off them and into this godforsaken dip in the landscape.

Clapping his hands together, he wondered where to start. May as well begin in The Arms. He turned round, took a step forward and stopped. The pub's sign had been replaced by a 'To Let' notice. He walked to the corner and looked off to the left.

The Castle was still going; in his day a few of the younger lot drank in there. A couple of figures were huddled out front. One looked up, sucking on the end of a cigarette. His eyes widened. 'Greg fucking Lang. What brings you back?'

He came to halt, flexed his fingers, angled his head. 'All right, Stevie. How's it going?'

The other man dropped the cigarette butt in the plant pot beside the table. 'Still living in the city, are you?'

'Aye.'

'Working?'

'Aye, this and that. My own stuff.'

Stevie's nostrils flared as he sniffed. 'Got any ciggies?'

Greg took a pack of Embassy from his jacket pocket. He wasn't sure who the other bloke was, but offered him all the same. A minor investment. Each man immediately produced a lighter; it was no use trying to get another person's cigarette going on Kilree's streets. The wind didn't allow it.

Greg lit one for himself, took a drag and blew smoke towards the doorway. 'Many in?'

'A few.' Stevie looked him up and down. 'Are you after anyone in particular?'

'Not really. When did the The Arms close?'

Stevie looked at his companion. 'Two, three years?'

'Nearer four.'

'Nearer four,' Stevie repeated, looking back at Greg. 'That's Gavin, by the way. Fergus' younger brother.'

Greg nodded. 'Thought you looked familiar. How is the big man? Still working the rigs?'

'Aye. Just gone out to the Gulf. Six month contract.'

Greg whistled. 'Jammy bastard.'

Stevie scraped a foot back and forth. 'You've not got any pills for sale, Greg?'

He shook his head. 'No.'

Stevie grimaced. 'Shame. You could have got rid of a few in there later. The usual guy's not been round yet.'

Greg dropped his cigarette end on the pavement. It trembled for an instant then rolled rapidly to the edge of the kerb where it dropped from sight.

There were less than ten people inside, two of them female. To his relief, he recognised one of them: Linda Woodhead. Curly black hair, cut short. She caught his eye and looked away. A memory surfaced. Late night, snogging her in a shop doorway. It hadn't led to anything. Her mate's hair was longer. A kind of pale orange, too. Greg took his hands out of his pockets, glad of the warmer air. The barman was waiting. Greg pointed to the end pump. 'Three pints of Deuchars, cheers.'

Immediate relief on Stevie and Gavin's faces. That's the last thing you get out of me, Greg thought, taking a tenner from his pocket. Once they'd sat down, he placed his hands on the table. 'Who's that with Linda?'

Stevie glanced across the pub, smirking. 'On the pull, Greg? You always were a total pussy-hound. She's called Stella.'

'You know her?'

'Course.'

'Does she have a fella?'

'Nothing regular.'

'Does she work?'

Stevie gave him a look.

'Yeah she does,' Gavin cut in. 'She managed to get a couple of shifts in the Spar.'

Stevie crossed his arms. 'Why are you asking?'

Greg took a slow sip, stretching the moment out, letting the men's curiosity grow. 'I'm starting a new business. Aimed at women. The right ones can earn cash – paid there and then.'

Stevie grinned. 'You're a pimp?'

'Fuck off. This is proper work.'

'Porn?'

Greg closed his eyes for a moment. 'Any more dick-head suggestions?'

'What then?'

'Linked to the beauty industry.'

Stevie frowned. 'Beauty industry? Like modelling or something?'

'It's to do with hairdressing.' He tipped his head in the girls' direction. 'Get them over. I'll explain.'

CHAPTER 6

Stella shot an uncertain look at Linda, who continued to stare at Greg. Stella's hand reached up and she touched the hair at the side of her head, as if seeking reassurance it was still there. 'Two hundred pounds?'

Linda tapped a nail against the rim of her glass. 'He's a dodgy bastard.'

'Piss off, Linda,' Greg sighed. 'This isn't dodgy.' Stella was in the periphery of his vision. He remembered chasing after girls with hair like hers in the playground. Yanking their ponytails and making them squeal.

'So...what?' Linda asked. 'You get out a pair of scissors and just,' she made a cutting motion with two fingers and turned to her friend. 'I would not be going off anywhere with Greg Lang.'

Greg took out a business card. Michelle had done a good job of printing them. Thick, with a top layer that looked like it had been varnished. He snapped the corner of it against the table. Quality. He spoke to Stella, not Linda. 'Here's who I represent. I don't have anything to do with that part of the process. But if you want, I'll book you in. They'll pay you cash and then give you a free haircut – you know, properly styled and all that. The person who does it is ex-Toni & Guy. You don't just get your ponytail lopped off and then shown back out on to the street.'

Stella picked the card up and studied it with interest. After a couple of seconds, Linda couldn't resist. She held out a hand. 'Let's have a look at one.'

Greg finished the rest of his pint. 'Sorry, Linda, there's no demand for black hair. Even if you did grow it long, plenty of chinkies are willing to sell theirs for peanuts.'

He stood up, relishing the crestfallen expression on her face. 'Call me,' he said to her mate as he turned towards the door. 'You won't regret it.'

He was almost back on the main road when his ears first caught it. That noise some bikes made when free-wheeling. Tickety-tickety-tickety-tickety. He lifted his chin reluctantly and coldness went straight down his collar. She flashed by not three feet away. An apparition from the past, hair streaming in the air. Long silvery-white strands that whipped and flexed. He stuck his chin back down as her bike carried her swiftly away, bulging panniers giving it extra momentum.

She was the weird woman who lived on her own up in the woods. Now he could no longer make out the bike's wheels: she seemed detached from the ground. Airborne with that hair startling the gloom behind her.

The community centre was at the other end of the high street. It hadn't changed much. A new ramp with railings leading up to the front entrance. The same fine grid of wire was embedded in the windows of the front doors. And there was still a bunch of youngsters away to the side, smoking. Greg smiled, making his way across the empty car park. As he got closer, he could hear a tinny buzzing. Wasps fighting in a baked bean tin. What, he wondered, was the point of playing music through your mobile?

'How's it going?' he announced, slouching against the hand rail and looking at the doors. He crossed one foot over the other, just to make sure his new Nikes were clearly visible. 'Mrs McMahon still running this place?' He saw suspicion on some faces, disinterest on others. 'She still go mental if you throw soggy bog-roll against the ceiling in the crapper?'

A few of the lads laughed. One asked: 'You from here,

then?'

He gave a slow nod while pursing his lips. I know what it's like for you, the movement said. 'Living in Glasgow now, thank fuck.' The answer had the effect he wanted: someone from the big city. A world away from this shithole. He considered how best to make his next move. Three of the girls had long hair. Two had it all tied up, but he could tell there was quite a bit there.

'What do you do in Glasgow?' This from the lad with the mobile phone that buzzed with mangled music.

Greg realised the question solved everything. 'Fashion industry. I'm kind of a spotter.'

'Like modelling?' one of the lads asked. 'Eve there's got big tits. She flashes them all the time.'

General laughter and a flurry of insults. Greg let them get on with it. Eve had her hair hanging down. Blonde, eighteen inches' worth. 'Hair,' he stated, letting the word hang there.

As expected, the girls started to look more interested.

'I represent a salon,' Greg continued. 'You girls know all about hair extensions?'

The music on the phone was turned up. Lads started resuming conversations. That was fine with Greg. He made his way closer to the cluster of females. 'We're looking for girls with fair hair. The longer, the better – '

'Excuse me, what's going on?' The voice came from behind him. It was firm, teacherly. Mrs bloody McMahon. Greg looked back. She was more hunched up than he remembered her. Greyer. But still alert, still firm on her feet. 'How are you, Mrs McMahon?'

Her face showed no recognition.

'It's Greg? Greg Lang? I used to come here when I was their age.' He flexed his knees and batted a hand back and forth. 'Demon at the ping-pong, I was. Remember me?'

Her face had relaxed, but only a little. 'I do. How are you, Greg?'

'Fine, thanks. You?'

'Not so bad. What brings you back?'

'Oh, just passing by. Thought I'd have a wander. Visit old haunts. The place hasn't changed.'

He could see suspicion lurking beneath her bright smile. The woman wasn't stupid. Just passing by: it was never going to wash with someone like her.

'Well, good to see you again, Greg. You lot? Time you were back in. Come on, now.' She started down the steps at the side of the ramp, focus now on the group, palms making scooping motions towards the doors. 'Lee, turn the music off, please. All of you, in we go.'

'Mrs McMahon, I'm not up to anything. Honest.' He tried to give her a reassuring grin, but she wasn't for making eye contact.

'I'm sure you're not Greg. But break time is over.'

He felt like a drug pusher at the school gates: it was what she obviously suspected. He fumbled for a card. 'I work for a salon in Glasgow. We're looking for – '

'That's very good, Greg. I'm glad you've done well for yourself. In we go now.'

The kids were filing past, one or two sending him smirks. Piss, he thought. I nearly had this cracked. As Mrs McMahon turned towards the steps, he felt the card being tugged from his fingers. He looked sideways. The one with the big tits was taking it, a pouty look on her face. He let go of it, flashed her a lopsided grin and stepped out of the way. 'Good to see you again, Mrs McMahon! And thanks for making me feel so welcome.'

Twenty minutes into the bus ride back to Glasgow, his phone rang. He didn't recognise the number and almost ignored the call. 'Yup?'

'It's Eve speaking. From outside the community centre earlier on?'

CHAPTER 7

He scrunched up the waxed-paper the burger had come in and dropped it in the empty carton of French fries. Why do it? he asked himself. I'll be hungry again in a couple of hours. But the housing estate he'd just spent the afternoon traipsing round wasn't exactly big on choice. A couple of cafes with pensioners sipping on mugs of tea. A fish bar whose windows had filmed over with grease.

'Shall I take your tray?'

He looked at the young lass in her nice clean outfit. 'Cheers.'

Her hair was tied back, forehead fully exposed. She lifted his formica tray from the table and turned. Long dark ponytail. It swished to the side as she walked away. Nice shine to it. Twenty inches, at least. He shook his head. Was a time, he reflected, when I'd have been checking out her arse. Now it's hair. Colour, thickness, condition, length. Value.

The last time he'd popped in to Mishi's, he'd asked Michelle to explain how it worked when someone came in to sell their hair. As he'd suspected, it had to be done properly.

The surface of hair, she'd explained, is covered in a protective layer of tiny scales, called cuticles. Collect it carefully, with every strand pointing in the same direction, and you're fine. Muck it up by lying some hair this way, some hair that, and the cuticles snag – that leads to it getting tangled and matted.

She'd pulled out a drawer and held up a long, narrow sheath of cellophane. 'This is one I collected this morning.'

Gregory had looked at the contents. The length of hair resembled a lustrous horse's tail – it even narrowed at the top where a smooth band secured it. A loop in the band went over a small plastic hook built into the top seam of the packet.

'That's what's known as cuticle intact,' she'd announced. 'Once it's been attached to the new owner, they can do what they want – perm it, blow dry it, curl it, plait it, braid it – just like it's their own. Look at the shine. Beautiful isn't it?'

He'd shrugged. 'Suppose so.'

'Suppose so?' Michelle had rolled her eyes. 'You sent the girl I collected it from.'

Greg had prodded the cellophane sheath. 'That salon: they send you this? To put the hair in?'

She'd nodded. 'Though, to be honest, wrapping it in cling film would do just as well.'

He tracked the staff member as she began to push the detritus of his meal through the opening at the top of a bin. It was a shame her hair wasn't a lighter shade; with the wages she would be getting from this place, she'd probably be keen for a bit of cash. He wiggled his phone out of the breast pocket of his denim jacket.

Three of the girls he'd given cards to earlier on were up for it: he'd booked them in there and then. Groups: they were best. If you could work on a bunch of them together, once one went for it, they all did. Michelle said six had turned up for their slots since Tuesday. Only one no-show. At this rate, he'd hit double figures for the week. Four hundred pounds per length of hair. After he deducted what the owners were paid and Michelle's share, he'd still have well over a grand of cash in his hand. He wanted to laugh.

His mind drifted on to the scenario he had rehearsed

so often in his head. Michelle, delighted and a little overwhelmed by how well he was doing. The graft he was putting in. The two of them sitting there, working out their profits. He pondered whether that evening would be too soon to float the suggestion her way. A celebratory drink. Not the pub, either. Somewhere more upmarket. He didn't mind paying. Not now they were practically business partners.

Michelle answered on the third ring. 'Greg, hiya! How's it going?'

'Good. Another three are coming your way. All booked in for Monday.'

'Three! You're a bloody machine, you are. Made for this.'

He grinned. 'Ah, well – '

'Where was this?'

'Little place near Tynthyre. About an hour away.'

'Are you still there?'

He was about to say no. He almost said he was just five minutes' walk away. But something made him stop. 'There now, aye.'

'OK, listen – I'm locking up in a few minutes. Today's Thursday. How about we speak tomorrow? We can sort out your money then.'

This would be good, he thought. He knew she liked a drink or two on a Thursday evening. He could surprise her: turn up and suggest they go for a couple. She'd probably say yes.

When he reached the salon, Andrea was stepping out the door, her coat on. The sign said closed. 'All right?'

Her head twisted, surprise all over her face. 'Greg.' Her eyes cut back to the salon's dim interior.

'She still in there?'

'Yes, but – but she's busy. With a client.'

He placed a hand on the door to stop it clicking shut and raised a finger to his lips. 'You get on home. I'll wait for her.'

She seemed unwilling to get out of his way. 'If you're sure. I mean, I don't know how long she'll be...'

He squeezed past her, keeping his voice low. 'I'll read the magazines, no bother. See you tomorrow.'

She stood on the pavement looking back at him with a strange expression. He wondered, for a moment, if she was building up to saying something. Asking what he was doing for the rest of the evening, maybe. But then she gave a tight smile and hurried off down the street.

He let the door click shut. The front of the salon was lit by just a couple of soft ceiling lights and he looked about for the switches. Far side of the room, by the doorway into the back area. He sauntered across and ducked his head through. It smelled strongly of weird candles. The door to the treatment room was closed and he could hear soft music plinking away on the other side. Floaty and insubstantial. Michelle said something, but he couldn't make it out. A female voice made an approving noise.

To his side was a work station: desktop computer, printer, files, folders and trays. Something started buzzing and he stepped closer. Michelle's phone. Andrea's name was showing on the screen. The call went to answer phone after two more buzzes.

He examined the printer – she'd bought one of those multipurpose ones. There were a few print outs sitting in the tray and he lifted the top one out. The logo immediately caught his eye. Felicity's. The tail of the 'y' turned into a gently undulating line that ran beneath the rest of the letters. The end of the line splayed out into countless thin lines. Hair, he realised. It was meant to look like hair. He read the opening words.

Hi Michelle,

Lovely work with sourcing the extensions! I'm so surprised you've managed to secure us such quality, so fast. The samples you sent last week were exactly what we need – demand down here is going through the roof. For that quality, we'll take whatever you send.

Which brings me to the question of prices. As agreed in our initial conversation, rates are six-hundred pounds for every twenty-four inches, with twenty pounds for each inch after that.

Greg stopped reading. Six-hundred pounds for every twenty-four inches? That's not what Michelle had told him. Fifty-fifty, she'd said. And on a rate of four-hundred pounds per twenty-four inches.

He sent a venomous glance at the treatment room's door. She was shafting him. Like he was some dick-head.

He lifted the sheet and continued to read.

'You mentioned you've sourced another six so far this week, with more anticipated. Well done! It is so refreshing to work with a supplier who actually delivers. So many just talk the talk. And so glad to hear you like the target and bonus proposal. For us, it shows real commitment on your part.

Let's speak after this weekend when things calm down a bit down here.

Take care,

Mia xxx

Greg looked at the door again. She'd said nothing about any bonus. There he was, slogging round grim estates while she was back here, cleaning up. She hadn't even told them who was actually bringing all the hair in. The realisation made his breathing speed up: he was no better than Andrea. Or was he worse? She'd probably been paid the right amount for her hair. He should kick the door open and ask what the fuck she was playing at. Bitch.

Clutching the piece of paper, he swivelled the chair round. When the door opened, she was getting a fucking mouth full, no messing. He waited a couple of minutes, catching the soft murmur of voices again during a lull in the music. No rush, he thought. I'll wait. His eyes went back to the sheet and he read it through again, dwelling on the figures the place down in London had quoted.

The fact she was doing him over the money could only mean one thing: he was nothing to her. She was using him. Getting him to do her work by dangling the chance of them...he shut the thought down as fast as he could. There were a few more lines beneath the person's signature.

By the way, a customer has given us a commission. (This happens very rarely!) She wants Russian Virgin quality, thirty-six inches, minimum. And it has to be very palest platinum. Also, the provider will need to be vegetarian, a non-smoker and –

The music from inside the treatment room lifted as the door began to open. He glimpsed the flicker of candles. Michelle was stepping out, a sleepy smile on her lips. She was doing up her blouse and her hair was all tousled. Greg sat motionless, all his attention on her face. He knew that face. That lazy-eyed look she always had just after sex.

She spotted him and both eyebrows shot up. 'Jesus, Greg, what are you – '

He felt himself rising, starting forward. Whoever was in the doorway behind her was dead. Fucking dead. The fucker's head was coming off.

Sheila's face appeared.

Greg came to a stop. He was blinking. Where was the bloke? There was no bloke. Only the pair of them.

'Greg, how come you're here?' Michelle glanced uneasily towards the front room. 'Where's Andrea?'

It came together in his head. Andrea's reaction when he'd shown up. The call to Michelle's mobile. It had been a warning. He didn't know what to do. Sheila and Michelle were just staring. 'You,' he said in a quiet voice. 'The two of you are – '

Michelle ran a quick hand through her hair. 'Shit. Why aren't you in Tynthyre? You said on the phone...'

It was making sense. Finally. He knew there was someone else. There always was. Sly bitch. The lying, sly bitch. 'I fucking knew it.'

'Greg...'

Greg. It was all she could manage. Just his name, said like an admission of guilt. 'All the shit you've been spouting. I fucking knew there was more to it.' He adopted a whining voice. 'We've grown apart. The spark has gone. It's just one of those things.' His fingers flexed in and out. 'I knew you were lying.'

'It wasn't this,' she said, eyes fixed on his. He glanced down at her open blouse and she immediately lifted a hand, searching for the buttons. 'We didn't plan this.'

'It's true,' Sheila chipped in. 'She was telling the – '

'Shut your fucking mouth.' Greg didn't even look at her. 'You fucking let me believe I was shit. Not good enough.' He took a step closer. 'But it's you who's the piece of shit.'

Their eyes looked back at him. They filled his vision. Eyes full of fear. The realisation released a wave of energy through him. He raised a fist, looked at it. There was no one to fight. No one he could attack. He dropped a shoulder and slammed the heel of his hand into the wall right beside her head. 'Fuck!'

She let out a little cry of terror and they both shrank back. The plaster had dented, a curved crack running above it. Seeing the damage made him feel good. He slammed his hand into it again and the thin board fractured. He could see the batons behind it. Cheap shit partition wall. Sheila pulled Michelle back into the treatment room as he hooked his fingers into the hole and ripped a chunk of wall away. Yes! Fucking yes! He turned sideways and kicked out with his heel. It went straight through.

The door slammed on him. He swung the flat of his hand against it and felt the whole thing shudder. He did it again and they whimpered behind their flimsy defence. It felt great. He raised a foot and was about to boot if off its hinges when he stopped. What was the point? What was the fucking point? Humiliation was sucking away his anger.

He felt so stupid. Michelle starting up with a lass. Not a man, a lass. He retreated to the chair and sat down again. There was a lump in his throat. He exhaled noisily. 'Jesus.' His temples were pounding, legs shivering violently.

'Greg?' Michelle's voice from the other side of the door. 'Greg, are you there?'

He stared at the floor. The piece of paper was lying there. It must have fallen from his hand as he'd stood. He picked it up again. A supplier who actually delivers. Targets and bonus proposal. She had set him up, let him run around like some stupid puppy. His chest churned like it used to when he was little. Just before he cried.

'Greg, we need to – '

'Just fuck off!' He side-swiped the computer monitor as he walked from the room. It clattered to the floor behind him. The table of magazines were to his side. All those bitches with their pouting lips, glossy hair and perfect faces. Smiling at him like they were nice. He launched the table against the wall, tugged the front door open and blundered off up the street.

CHAPTER 8

The road started rising more steeply. Soon, the engine of the bus began to labour and the driver pressed in the clutch to change down a gear. For a brief moment they were free-wheeling up a slope. Greg frowned: the world felt the wrong way round. Free-wheeling upwards. Then the clutch re-engaged and the bus begrudgingly lurched forward.

Greg moistened the end of his finger and dipped it in the little plastic bag once again. He smeared the fine powder against his gums and, seconds later, the blood behind his eyeballs surged. Keep going at it like this, he thought, and there'd be none left to sell to Stevie. Give a shit. That wasn't the reason he was going back.

They reached the village where he'd grown up but Greg stayed on the rear seat of the bus. Letting the engine idle, the driver unfolded a newspaper and began to read. Greg felt like his skull was shrinking. Or brain expanding. He blinked. Everything was so sharp. He relished the feeling. Like he had enhanced powers. The engine's thrum reverberated in his ears, more like a sound effect playing on a loop. Artificial. He found he could focus on individual noises within it. The deep hollow notes of the exhaust, the harder sounds of engine parts rubbing together. A percussive ticking from a loose window frame. They all became entwined, then slowly separated again. He bobbed his head in time.

Outside, the high street was still. Like the entire place was in hibernation. With a sigh, the driver refolded his paper, put it aside, flicked the indicator down and set off. The road was narrower as it left the village, winding its way up the valley, trees forming a wall on both sides. Pine, birch, others Greg had no names for. He watched carefully: she lived somewhere up in the woods. There was a track, if he remembered rightly, near a roadside warning sign about deer.

As soon as it came into view, he pinged the bell and long-stepped his way down the empty aisle. The driver pulled over, made some comment about the benefits of fresh air and released the doors. Greg nodded in reply as he jumped down on to the verge.

Cold air and a quietness beyond the grumble of the bus. The track was about thirty metres further along. He reached for his cigarettes as the bus resumed its lonely journey. Lighting one up, he set off, dismayed at how slow it was on foot and how fast his cigarette was shrinking in the chill breeze. Once on the track itself, he took another dab of powder. For energy: no telling how far it was to the place she lived. Could be a right trek. As a schoolboy, he'd heard rumours it was way out in the forest. But that was according to other kids – and they had little legs. She was meant to have been a teacher, once. Or was it a scientist? Biology or something.

The woods were still. The occasional chitter of a bird, but not much else. He always imagined it would be buzzing with noise. The odd lull in the wind gave smells a chance to announce themselves. Musky and damp. He remembered being pinned down once by an older lad. It had been in the far corner of the school playing field, where the teachers couldn't see. Wet mud had been smeared in his face, up his nose. It was that smell again; he didn't like it.

She'd first started appearing in the village when he was about twelve or thirteen. Word soon spread that she'd bought a forester's lodge nearby. So, for almost sixteen years, she'd lived out here on her own. Sometimes folks walking their dogs spotted her picking her way between the trees, head bowed as she collected plants. Talking to herself. Some of the lads – the ones who liked making camps and stuff – claimed they'd even seen her up among the branches, like a proper freak.

The scissors in his pocket banged lightly against his thigh with each step. He patted the roll of cling-film in the jacket pocket as he pictured the letter from Mishi's salon, the one he'd walked off with after catching Michelle and Sheila together. Two thousand pounds for a thirty-six inch length of the palest platinum. He had a tape measure in his pocket, too. Even though what he'd seen hanging down the old woman's back was easily long enough.

Michelle could get fucked: he'd deal direct with the place in London from now on. And this woman's hair would be his way in – all the proof they needed that it was him who could source the stuff. Not that lying slag in her salon.

He could hear a knock-knocking sound. Wooden and hollow. Not a tune, but still musical. It reminded him a bit of the mad rhythm going on in the bus, only slower. More kicked back and relaxed. The track curved left and the trees shrank back to leave a clearing. There it was. A small wooden bungalow thing with little windows and a spindly metal chimney. A wisp of smoke was being erased by the breeze. The funny noise was coming from a row of wooden tubes hanging from the branches of a nearby tree. At the end of the building a lean-to roof gave cover to a neat stack of logs. She had no fence, but you could tell where the garden started: neat rows of vegetables were growing immediately before the property. Clumps of leaves, some dark green, others a purplish-red. Lighter green bobbles clinging to long stems. He looked closer. Brussel sprouts! He never knew that's how they looked in the wild.

As he approached the door, he thought about the letter, the need for the hair to come from a vegetarian. This woman was perfect – the best he was likely to find, no doubt about it.

Something was arrowing towards him from the nearby trees. He turned his head, shoulders hunching. A bird, wings beating rapidly. It angled up at the last second to alight on the edge of the roof. Leaning forward, it peered inquisitively down at him. Its plumage was oddly colourful and he wondered if it was a woodpecker; weren't they meant to have green or blue or something in their feathers?

It was definitely watching him. He half-raised a hand to scare it away, but then realised he was visible from the hut. What if it was some kind of pet? Instead, he approached the door and knocked on it softly. To be polite. It opened surprisingly fast. Had she been watching him from inside? Probably.

There was a step up to the door. Enough so she could look down at him with eyes that were sharp and impatient. Close up, he could see her face was criss-crossed by a web of incredibly fine wrinkles. Totally covered. Yet she wasn't ancient. It was like the skin of some old pirate – what you got after a life out in the wind and rain and sun.

There was something else about her that took a moment for him to put his finger on: no make-up. None what-so-ever.

'Yes?' She was frowning.

'Good afternoon.' He tried a friendly grin, but his face was cold and it felt like he was bearing his teeth at her.

'Are you lost?'

She was one of those people whose age seemed to shift every second. One moment, she could have been early fifties. But when she spoke, the etches in the skin around her lips deepened. Suddenly, she jumped into her late sixties. She spoke as if she was in a hurry, like he was stopping her from doing something far more important.

'I'm here with an offer, actually. Cash. Half now – '

She reached out a skeletal hand to start closing the door. Her ponytail swung into view. Easily three feet long. The colour of bark from a silver birch.

The door started to swing shut, so he stepped up and met it with his palm. 'You haven't let me explain.'

Fear flashed in her eyes, but only for a second. 'Take your hand off, I'm not interested.'

She thinks I'm a door-to-door salesman, he thought. She thinks she can bark an order at me and off I'll scurry. 'You're not being very nice.'

The comment appeared to wrong-foot her. She gave up trying to force the door shut. Crossing her arms, she regarded him more carefully. 'You want money. Is that it?'

He heard a scratching and looked up. The bird had edged its way along the gutter and was now almost directly above him. He lowered his hand and smiled. 'You're not listening. It's me offering you the money.'

'I don't want any money.' She gestured at the room behind her. 'I have what I need. I don't want anything more.'

How, he thought, is that possible? You live in a fucking shack. Probably don't even have electricity. He let his eyes drift up to her hairline. 'You have very beautiful hair.'

She looked at him in silence.

The bird's presence was an irritation. He flung a hand up at it. 'Piss off!'

It jumped back, wings fluttering violently to gain height. As it vanished over the roof, his eyes settled on her once again. 'I'd like you to sell it to me.'

The forest surrounding them seemed suddenly hushed. Her lips parted in disbelief. 'Pardon?'

'Your hair, I'd like you to sell it to me.'

Her face went slack. She looked on the point of throwing up. 'My hair?' she croaked. Her head shook in horror.

He nodded back. 'I'll pay you for it.'

She shook her head more forcefully. The pleading in her eyes fed his sense of strength. He stepped fully up, filling her doorway, forcing her back.

'Please,' she whispered. 'Just leave.'

But he stepped into her home and pushed the door shut behind him. 'That's better, now I have two hundred – '

Without warning, she darted to the side, hand slamming down on a work surface. She whirled to face him, a small pair of scissors held before her. The blades barely cleared her clenched fist. 'Get out!'

Her voice surprised him. So packed with venom. Like he was there for her new-born baby. She was wearing a thick jumper with buttons in a line along her right collar bone. Her drab, ankle-length skirt was swaying slightly. He wanted to laugh as he produced his scissors and snipped the air with their seven-inch blades. 'I win.'

'Just get out! Now!'

You're exactly like Mrs McMahon, he thought. People like you, you think your best school mistress voice will solve anything. Maybe it does when you're returning stuff to a shop. Or complaining about a bill. Stupid bitch, though, if she thinks I'm leaving without her hair. 'Right. This is how we're going to – '

For an elderly woman, she was quick. Not just on her feet, the speed of her hand, too. Her fist connected with his upper arm and a white hot needle shot through it. She's stabbed me, he realised. She's fucking stabbed me! He could see the handle protruding from his arm. Then his own fingers flexed and his shoulder jerked back. Both pairs of scissors fell to the floor.

She lunged for them with one hand and he had to bring a knee up to try and drive her back. It connected with her shoulder. Claw-like fingers latched on to his belt and they went down together. She hardly touched the rug before transforming into a shrieking, writhing mass of limbs. An elbow hit him in the throat. A heel connected with his knee. He tried to get a hand on her throat, but she twisted to the side. Next thing, her fingers were at his eyes, digging and tearing. He squeezed them shut and drove a fist at the sound of her growl. The noise abruptly changed to a chocking sound, and from the pain across his knuckles, he guessed he'd caught her full in the teeth. But still she didn't stop. Another impact to his chest as she scrabbled back. Then a kick set one ear singing. Tears filling his eyes, he could just make her out as she started crawling away. Desperately, he stretched with his good arm. His fingers closed on the tip of her ponytail. He yanked as hard as he could and her head and shoulders snapped back. Grabbing her collar with his other hand, he looped the thick cord of hair round her throat and pulled with all his strength. Somehow, she kept crawling and he had to lean back, as if reigning in a wilful animal. Inch by painful inch, she struggled forward, breath a shallow rasp. He hung on, willing her unnatural strength to fade. The muscles in his arms felt like they were about to tear. One of her hands flailed at the low table beside an armchair, but the movement caused her other elbow to buckle and she hit the floor face-first. Getting a knee in the small of her back, he was able to put another loop around her neck. 'Stab me, you bitch,' he hissed into her ear through gritted teeth. 'Stab me?

The fight seemed to go from her. Rather than struggle, she held whatever she'd managed to snatch from the table against her forehead. Even though her tongue had started pressing from between her lips, she began trying to whisper. What was she doing? Praying? Pray all you want, he thought, keeping the loops tight. He watched as her face grew more and more purple. Still he kept the pressure up. Slowly, her fingers loosened and, once she became still, he relaxed his grip.

Her tongue retracted and her head lolled forward until it touched the floor. The object slipped from her slack fingers. A letter opener or something. He let her hair go and got unsteadily to his feet. Had that really just happened? Fucking hell, it had all been so fast. Still breathing heavily, he tottered over to a window and looked outside. The first thing he noticed was the tops of the trees violently thrashing around; he wondered if a storm was about to blow in. Then he checked the track. Empty. His ear felt like a beacon, throbbing hotly. It was being echoed by sharper pain that pulsed in his arm. Was he dripping blood all over the place? Eyes widening, he checked the floor: nothing. He lifted his fingers, but they were dry. The hole in his sleeve was tiny, hardly any blood visible around it.

He turned to where she lay, still not sure in his head. She was motionless, head turned to the side, eyes half-open. The fucking psycho bitch. She'd gone mad, nearly killed him. He stepped closer, tempted to swing a foot at her. Instead, he took another dab of powder from his bag, waited for it to kick in and then looked around.

The place was weird. From the slim rafters hung bunches of dried flowers and withered stems of plants. Nestled in the far corner was a wood-burning stove, a wicker basket of logs beside it. A couple of tables were covered in piles of books – old-looking things, some of them massive. She'd kept the shelves on the walls free for jars. Rank after rank of them, all possible shapes and sizes. Pickles, he thought. Like his gran used to make. But when he took a closer look, the things he saw hanging in the pale yellowish liquid made him shiver. Dead frogs, earthworms, fat-bodied spiders. In one was a bat, black-paper wings shrouding its furred body. The next few contained beetles. Beside them were what could have been tongues – from sheep or deer. He didn't know. 'You fucking freak,' he whispered, stepping back to examine a massive framed parchment. Odd symbols below a line of moons that went from fingernail thin to a perfect circle and back again. There were words, too. No language he recognised. Maybe messages or instructions from a long time ago.

He looked about for a television, or anything electrical. Nothing, just like he'd suspected. Not even light-bulbs. Lanterns hung from various places, but all of them were dead. Most of the light was shining in from large windows set in the roof. At the far end of the room there was a bed, and beside it, a stool and dressing table. Attached to the wall above it was an ornately-framed mirror. Wondering what it might be worth, he walked over. But the gold was just paint. Laid out on the dressing table were a few hand mirrors and several brushes and combs. He remembered how fast things went out of control when he told her what he wanted. Her hair. He could picture her sitting here, brushing it, dividing it, arranging it. Admiring it. How many years had it taken her to grow it that long?

He searched about for his scissors.

CHAPTER 9

The priest waited for more, but the man had stopped speaking. Over by the altar, Mrs Reynolds had tipped the vacuum on its side. Her fingers probed at the parts of the machine that spun and whirred. He hoped the thing was unplugged.

Looking silently down was the figure of Christ. The patch of sunlight had slipped lower and was now a band across the figure's torso, left arm and both legs. The curving rib cage and slit-like wound with its trickle of blood. The priest closed his eyes for a moment. In his mind, the story was like mould-tinged fruit in a bowl: asking questions would only fan its spores, spread its corruption. But he had to know. 'Gregory Lang: he told all this to that contact of yours, the toggy?'

From the corner of his eye, he saw the man nod.

The priest made sure to whisper. 'He strangled her with her own hair?'

The man nodded again.

'And after that?'

The man reached to his side for the attaché case. The loose buckles clinked slightly as it was opened and the priest – for one fearful moment – thought the man was about to produce the murdered woman's hair. But when the visitor's hand lifted, it was holding a magazine. *Snapped!*

'This is the latest issue. The one I was talking about.' He opened the cover with practised ease. 'On page five we run a feature known among the staff as 'Damsel In Distress'. A female interest story – a movie star being messily divorced, someone admitting to anorexia, that kind of thing. We were going with the Maggy Wallace murder – a kind of look back at her life and summary of the latest findings. Or lack of them. But then Mandy Cost went out that second-floor window.' He flicked a few pages over. 'Here. As I said, we only printed a few images – the ambulance crew shots and the broken window, mainly.'

Holding the magazine by its corners, the priest examined it at arm's length. What he saw shocked him. He knew images used in the press were becoming more extreme; they were competing with what circulated on the internet. But still. The main shot was of the second-floor window. What would have been someone's bedroom when the building had been a home.

Mandy Cost was visible behind a jigsaw of glass that was starting to explode out into the air. The priest could immediately see that her long hair was gone. The outline of her neck and skull was clear. She looked vulnerable. Exposed. Both palms were visible; held up as if to fend off the mass of jagged shards. The priest couldn't stop his eyes from trying to seek out her face. The need to know what she'd been thinking at that terrible moment.

But a section of glass obscured her eyes. What it didn't conceal was a mouth wide with terror. He focused on that dark spot and imagined the shriek she must have made. How long did it last? A second, no more. He imagined the unforgiving pavement zooming up to fill her vision. The thud as she landed.

He looked to the smaller images: a blanket laid over the body, one paramedic crouched beside it, another staring at the camera with a disbelieving expression. Behind them all, in the doorway to the salon, was a woman in a white tunic with one hand covering her mouth. He realised all the ground-floor windows were full of faces; staff and customers jostling for a view.

Guiltily, the priest moved on to a pair of shots of the second floor window. In one, the glass was intact and a shadowy silhouette was visible behind it. In the other most of the glass was missing. A before and after.

The final shot was of an ambulance pulling away, a cluster of people walking in its wake, smart phones held at the vehicle's rear.

He flicked through the next few spreads, stopping about half way. A headline stilled his hand. Maggy's Murder Mystery. A grainy photo of a high street. From the cars, he could tell it was decades old. She was looking over her shoulder, face gaunt and hostile, as she strode away from the camera. She wore a plain dun-green jumper and khaki dungarees. A silvery ponytail hung to the small of her back. 'And this is where Maggy Wallace ended up,' the priest stated sadly, 'once something better came in.' He looked at the lady's face a moment longer. There was no denying she had sharp – even cruel – features. But it also seemed obvious she hadn't consented to her photograph being taken.

The priest glanced at the man. Was he really who he said he was? Or was he here trying to fish for information? Eek one last story out at Mandy's expense? One that involved him? A thought occurred and, realising the man wasn't watching, the priest flicked to the inside cover. There, a panel listed all the magazine's staff, starting with the Editor and Deputy Editor. Below that was the title, Picture Editors, followed by several names. 'I'm sorry, I don't think you mentioned your name.'

The man continued looking straight ahead. 'Nigel.'

'Nigel...?'

'Crowther.'

The name matched one from the magazine's staff panel. Closing the cover, the priest thought for a moment. 'Correct me if I'm wrong, but – earlier – did you not say that the toggy person who took these shots – '

'Joe Sullivan.'

'– that Joe Sullivan worked in partnership with Mandy Cost?'

'Yes. In fact, it was Joe who got the very first photos of Mandy when she had the extensions put in.'

'Had they set that up that, too?' the priest asked glumly. Why had Mandy never mentioned the arrangement?

'Of course.'

'So they knew each other fairly well?'

Nigel Crowther scratched at an ear. 'You're wondering why he didn't help her?'

The priest placed the magazine beside him on the pew, glad it was no longer soiling his fingers. 'Is that unreasonable? To wonder that?'

'No, no, you're absolutely right. But Mandy and Joe's relationship wasn't normal. I mean, it wasn't based on feelings – affection and things like that. This sounds awful, I know, but it was just business. At least to Joe it was.'

The priest breathed deeply. His distaste wasn't relevant and it certainly wouldn't help. His job, at this point, was to simply listen. Ask the odd question. For him this was, he reflected grimly, just business.

'I can tell from your silence you're not happy,' Nigel announced, voice hardly audible once more. 'But these pictures – they're currency. They have value. Sales of this issue are the highest we've had in years. Literally, people can't get a copy fast enough.'

'What did you pay Joe Sullivan for them?'

'Enough. Top-of-the-range car: that sort of amount.'

'But still a profitable deal for you.'

'Copies are flying off the shelves.'

'If someone has a taste for something that is unhealthy, is it right to carry on feeding them?'

His visitor lifted a shoulder. 'Questions like that, they do trouble me. They do. I know it's a horrible thing we're all caught up in. I can see that. But it works, from an economic view. Well, most of the time, it works. Pictures kept Mandy's profile high. That meant work for her. It also meant work for Joe. Me, too. And everyone at *Snapped!* Our customers get something they crave: glimpses of the famous. Whether wanting those glimpses is unhealthy, hey – what can I do? People love celebrities. Ever since Cleopatra, ever since…I don't know when.'

'But is it right?'

'Surely, people should be free to choose.'

'All freedom comes at a price,' the priest muttered. 'Regardless of that, Joe Sullivan valued getting those pictures over helping another human being.'

'He regrets that. Bitterly. But you need to know what went on between him and Mandy. It's all part of what's happening now.'

The priest sat back. 'Very well. What went on between Joe and Mandy?'

Nigel Crowther stared down at the magazine on his lap. Then his chin lifted. 'It was less than a fortnight ago when Joe rang me. That call was about when Mandy was going to have the hair extensions put in.'

CHAPTER 10

'Hi Nigel, Joe Sullivan here.'

'What have you got for me, Joe?'

'Brand new look for Mandy Cost.'

'Brand new? Meaning what?'

'Different clothes, completely different hair. Total make-over. You'll hardly recognise her.'

'Very interesting.'

'Loads of choice, too. She's coming out of her favourite salon: Felicity's in Mayfair. Pausing on the top step to check something on her phone; full body and facial close-ups. Then getting into her car with thigh and cleavage showing.'

'How much?'

'Enough to send teenage lads across the country scuttling off to their bedrooms.'

Nigel Crowther laughed. 'Apart from you, who else?'

'Only me.'

'We're talking an exclusive for *Snapped*, then?'

'Absolutely. You've got first refusal. As usual, mate.'

'OK, thanks. Can you give me a link? I'll have a look and we can talk prices.'

'I'm taking the shots tomorrow.'

A slight pause. 'Tomorrow? Oh, I get it. You're a crafty bastard, Joe. She's given you the nod on this?'

'Indeed she has.'

'You sure you're not slipping it to her? No need to be

modest; most blokes would.'

'Just business, mate. Just business.'

'Deadline's tomorrow evening for the next issue.'

'That's why you'll have the shots by two in the afternoon, latest.'

'Lovely. Speak tomorrow, then.'

'Will do, cheers Nigel.' Joe Sullivan cut the call and dropped his phone on the cushion beside him. 'Sorted. I reckon he's good for at least four shots, maybe more. I've never heard him use the term 'very interesting' and not be.'

Mandy Cost took a delicate drag on her cigarette, lips contracting to a pout as she did so. She blew the smoke over her shoulder, away from where they were sitting. 'So a half-page, then? Possibly more?'

'Possibly more. You heard me promise him plenty of cleavage and thigh.'

'Not a problem. Lycra vest top and micro-skirt combi.'

'Trusty favourite.'

'Trusty favourite.'

'So, how dramatic is this new look going to be?'

She dropped the cigarette through the narrow opening at the top of a pillar-shaped ashtray on the coffee table. Leaning back in her seat, she fluffed out some straggles of collar-length auburn hair. 'This is going to be straightened. And I'm having it dyed to match the extensions. They're this incredible silvery colour.'

'Not blonde?'

'No, I wanted paler than that. Practically white. I've fancied it for a while, but it took ages to find the right shade and length. And I'm going for length – right down my back.'

'Lady Godiva look?'

'Who's she?'

He opened his mouth, then lifted a hand instead. 'Doesn't matter. Extensions, then?'

'Yes. Mia at Felicity's. It took her a few weeks, but she found me exactly what I wanted. So,' she ran a manicured nail along each eyebrow, 'I'll be keeping these dark.' A finger pointed to her mouth. 'Lips pale. Outfits black and figure-hugging. It's all about contrasts. Light and dark. Works for anything: coming out the gym, going to restaurants, anything. What do you think?' She sat back, eyes wide in expectation.

So needy, he thought. So dependent on approval. Her dad either starved her of affection or treated her like some little dolly. 'Sounds amazing.' He made himself nod. 'I mean, like, head-turning. Imagine you in heels, in a dark shimmery evening gown...shit.'

Her smile was huge. 'I'd have the hair up for formal stuff. With the length I'm getting I can have braids, plaits, all that. So, you like it?'

'Think it's a stroke of genius, Mands. It can be classy or not, you know?'

'What do you reckon with my tits?' She cupped one with each hand. 'I was wondering whether to go a size or two bigger.'

He looked briefly at the milky valley emerging from her top. 'You always said surgery was a red line. Botox, yes. Teeth, yes.' He nodded at her full lips. 'Whatever it is that gives you the sexy pout.'

'I know, I know. But...you're not thinking...' She let her breasts fall back into place. 'It's just, sometimes, I feel old. Am I looking old to you?'

He stopped himself from checking his watch. She'd been here a good ten minutes. From the street outside came the noise of someone yelling. Probably over a parking space. A workman's drill drowned it out. 'No way. What are you?' He knocked a few years off the figure in his head. 'Early twenties?'

She batted a hand. 'Charmer. Twenty-six. That's what I mean, Joe. I wanted to have my retirement pot by twenty-five. I always said if I started to think about surgery, it was time to call it a day. And now here I am thinking about it.'

He considered her comment. She was his best client.

How many times did she put opportunities his way? Loads. She couldn't quit. Not yet. 'You've got years ahead of you, Mands. Years. And if you decide a bit of work's needed at some point down the line, that's your decision.'

'Yeah, I suppose.' Her phone went and she checked the screen before accepting the call. 'Hi Wayne. Is it? Right...OK. I'll be out in two.' She lowered the device. 'That's my driver. I need to go.' She gave him a school-girl smile. 'Of course, if that escape route's still open, I can forget about surgery.'

She kept the smile but her eyes waited eagerly for his reply.

'My little bolt-hole out in the country?' He dinked a forefinger in her direction and gave her a wink. 'You and me, babe. Away from all this shit. Wouldn't it be great?'

She got to her feet. Beyond the drone of traffic outside, a siren started to wail. 'Views across the ocean and collecting driftwood off the beach for our own fires.'

He sat back. 'And I'll teach you to surf. In the summers you can make jam and sell it to the tourists.'

'God, stop it. Sounds like heaven, that place. Time to go, I'm late already.'

'Where are you meant to be?'

She grimaced. 'Bloody accountant. He's got some new scheme. Listen, one o'clock tomorrow, yeah?'

He made to stand but she patted the air before his face. 'Don't be late. I'll give you a wave from the window when I'm ready. Second floor.' Bending down, she planted a kiss on his cheek.

Joe continued looking at the door to his flat after she'd closed it behind her. What was going on with her? He still couldn't figure it out. The bolt-hole had originally been just a throw-away, mildly flirtatious, line he'd come out with.

It had been on a night when she'd gone to a restaurant where he had a contact among the kitchen staff. As soon as she'd emerged at the end of the night, he'd stepped from the neighbouring doorway – and his camera died on him.

Relieved, she'd started looking around for her driver, but he was nowhere to be seen.

So there the two of them were like a right pair of lemons: her with no car, him with no means of taking her picture. Seeing the funny side, they got chatting. He'd ended up giving her a lift home on the back of his motorbike. She'd laughed at how old and battered it was, convinced people like him were making a fortune from the photos they took. He'd countered with something about her paying a driver who didn't even show up.

Outside her place, conversation moved to the surreal celebrity world they both operated in – the chased and the chasers, each needing the other. He'd agreed it could be crap, skulking outside places until the early hours, hoping for a lucky shot. She'd agreed it was a constant hassle being tailed by snappers, sometimes shouting hurtful stuff to provoke a reaction.

'Who knows,' he'd said, taking his helmet off. 'One day, maybe you'll let me take you off this merry-go-round. We can go somewhere you can hear the sea and just sit back and relax.'

She'd stared at him for a second. 'You know somewhere like that, then?'

He'd almost said no. But sensing an opportunity, he gazed down at the visor of his helmet and lowered his voice. 'A little place I've got. Nothing flash. It's the location that's priceless.'

'Have you got a business card?' she'd replied.

The next day, she'd rung him with a suggestion. She'd feed him photo opportunities; he'd cut her a percentage of whatever the images sold for. The arrangement had worked like a dream. But she'd never forgotten about the bolt hole. Sometimes, it was like a comfort blanket she clung to.

He reached beneath the coffee table and pulled a small drawer out.

Comfort blanket? Mirage, more like. She might be able to see something, but nothing was really there. He had no bolt-hole out on the Norfolk coast. When she'd started pressing him for details, he'd ended up describing a place he'd once rented. It hadn't been for long – just a few days to clear his head, wander the beaches with his camera. The owner had mentioned you sometimes saw porpoises off the coast. Certainly, the walls of the little lodge were adorned with photographs of them cutting the surface of the sea at dawn or dusk. There were other wildlife shots, too. Various types of seagull, clusters of wading birds and lonely hawks suspended in the sky.

He took the thin box out of the drawer. Its lid was inlaid with mother-of-pearl.

It was her intentions that confused him. In the imaginary life she so liked to linger over, were they just friends? Was that how she saw them? Surely, if you were living in a little one-bedroom beach shack with a bloke, it must involve shagging? Not that he particularly fancied her, but she'd never even asked about bedrooms. So, in her dream, were they just companions? He knew she was never single – but he also knew her succession of boyfriends was chosen primarily for the media coverage they might generate. He wasn't convinced she actually slept with half of them.

He lifted the lid of the box and regarded the items nestling in the layer of moulded foam. The syringe was glass, the plunger surgical steel. He removed the small ceramic container that contained his heroin.

With Mandy's job safely lined up for the next day, he could kick back, take it easy. As he tapped granular powder into a miniature crucible, he gave a wry smile. With the amount he'd blown on this stuff over the years, he probably could have afforded a nice place by a beach.

CHAPTER 11

'Sullivan, you little weasel, tell me your secret.'

Joe smiled to himself. It was five days since the full page feature of Mandy's new look had appeared in *Snapped!* The difference those extensions made...it had been more than dramatic. In the first forty-eight hours, loads of other publications had got in contact, begging if he had any other shots for sale. His name was now on all the picture editors' lips.

He looked at the scowling man beside him. Andy Burrell was ex-Army and, Joe had to admit, slightly scary. The bloke always wore combat gear when on a job – even if it was in the West End of London.

Joe turned slightly, planted his feet a little wider and gave a thrust of his hips. 'It's quite simple, Andy. She just can't get enough.'

The other photographers let out a begrudging chorus of chuckles.

'She tells me everything,' Joe continued. 'Her entire schedule. Just for the odd ride on my truncheon of love.'

'Bollocks,' Andy retorted. 'You've got some dirt on her. Some sordid shit she can't afford to ever have seen.'

Someone at the end of the group spoke. 'You don't get more sordid than that home video her old boyfriend took. Have you gone on the internet to see it? Jesus, some of the positions he bends her into.'

'Seen it?' Joe said. 'Andy takes it to bed every night.'

More laughter.

Andy leaned in on Joe. 'Very funny, Sullivan,' he murmured. 'But you still haven't said.'

The threat of violence was like a smell wafting from the other man. Joe said nothing: he knew silence would torment him further.

'What did *Snapped!* pay you for the shots?' someone else asked. 'I heard it was twenty-five grand.'

'Only twenty-five?' Leaving his response hanging, he turned his attention to the night club's entrance. It was owned by an ex-member of the England football team who obviously had a very good address book: practically the entire squad had turned up for the opening night party. Them, their wives and girlfriends: the web would be awash with images by the time next morning's commuters started checking their smart phones. Joe checked his watch.

Two in the morning. The night editors would be expecting something soon for the online editions. Sure enough, the security staff beneath the entrance canopy began to move aside as a couple emerged. Joe pressed against the waist-high barrier. The flash and whir of cameras filled the air.

'Looking lovely tonight Mrs Coe!'

'Over here, love. Quick smile!'

'Mark – you and your wife – let's see a kiss!'

Joe recognised him as a midfielder. The wife had been a singer in a girl band, but that was years back. C listers, at best. They did the obligatory pause, him with an arm loosely around her waist, she with her hair flung back and a sultry look on her face. He fired off a few shots before they vanished into the first of the waiting courtesy cars, their brief taste of fame over for the night.

The usual procession then followed: footballers, soap star actors, a couple of TV chefs, a sprinkling of model types, a comedian turned chat-show host. Joe's camera clicked away with all the rest.

At two-forty, Mandy stepped out. Joe found himself

thinking it again: her new look was a stroke of genius. Immediately, the photographers' calls picked up a level. She had on a black satin dress, sleeveless with a slit running to the top of her right thigh. The front collapsed in rippling folds, low enough so her tits were nearly falling out.

But it was her hair that did it. That was what set her apart from all the women.

She'd had it looped in coils that teetered on top of her head. A collection of thinner strands hung loose, and all of it seemed to shimmer in the camera flashes, the near-whiteness of it like something from another world. An exotic life-form that somehow was, and wasn't, part of her.

The photographer by his side spoke with a thick voice. 'Imagine reaching up and freeing that lot. Feeling it thumping down on your naked chest.'

The comment caused a flash of realisation in Joe's head: she'd done it. She was a living, walking, sex fantasy. And now she'd be worth a fortune.

Mandy soaked it up for a few seconds, her eyes searching about. She spotted Joe and an eyebrow lifted a fraction. Then she spoke into a security guard's ear. Almost reverently, he ushered her towards the open doors of the nearest car.

A new couple appeared beneath the canopy and the camera lenses swung in their direction. Minutes later, Joe felt his phone start to vibrate. He whipped it out: Mandy. Still taking shots, he pressed the mobile to his ear. 'You made the rest look like sacks of shit.'

'Really? Do you think?'

But from the breathless excitement in her voice, he knew she was aware of it, too.

'And coming out on your own like that? Very very clever.'

She said something else.

'You'll have to speak up, it's all going off back here.'

'Can you take a look around?' she said more loudly.

'How do you mean?'

'Just, I don't know, check the street.'

'For what?'

'Anyone kind of unusual.'

'Unusual? I don't get you.'

'A woman. See if you can spot a woman on her own. I think I might be being stalked.'

'What kind of a woman?'

'Like a bag lady woman. Homeless or something. I've spotted her a few times now.'

Not wanting to lose his position, Joe quickly looked about. 'Can't see anyone – apart from us lot. What does she look like?'

'I don't know. I've only glimpsed her. But I think she's bald. Chemotherapy or something. Probably after money for her treatment.'

CHAPTER 12

'It's open.' Joe watched Mandy's grainy image disappear from the intercom's little screen. He glanced at his watch. Five-twenty in the afternoon. Odd time for her to be showing up at his door. Not that he minded: not now she was riding high.

Tying his long straggly hair back with a black band, he did a quick scan of the front room. As usual, it was clean and tidy. He couldn't stand mess. The crumb-laden plate on the coffee table was carried through to the little galley kitchen.

After pressing the button on the kettle, he headed back into the living room. He'd just had time to put some music on when she gave her usual double-tap. Opening the door, he felt the smile on his face collapse. She looked gaunt with worry.

'Come on in.' He stepped back. 'You all right, Mands?'

She came to a stop in the middle of the room and removed her head scarf. Light from the halogen ceiling bulbs caught in the silvery tresses as they tumbled down her back. It would have been sell-able. A fine art print. Something drenched in beauty, unlike the shitty snaps he peddled for a living. He wanted to freeze time, wind it back and get the shot.

But she was already folding herself into the armchair, knees off to the side.

He hovered before her. She had a troubled look on her

face and – for a second – he wondered if she was playing for effect. 'Mands?' Her eyes lifted and he could immediately tell she wasn't. 'What's up?'

A car horn beeped, others quickly joined in. An outbreak of aggressive squabbling that gradually ebbed.

'When did I last see you?' She sounded like she was coming round in a hospital bed.

He perched on the edge of the sofa. 'Two nights back, wasn't it? Saturday: when you came out of Right Half's with your hair up.'

Now staring at the floor, she nibbled the edge of a thumbnail. 'That's it. Was that two nights ago? I called you, didn't I, from the car?'

'That's right. Listen, do you want a coffee or something?'

'I mentioned someone to you. A woman.'

He slid down onto the sofa seat. 'Yeah. I looked around for you. No one was hanging about.'

'I think I'm being stalked. By her.' She threw an anxious glance at him.

'How do you mean stalked?'

'I keep seeing her, Joe.' She started a chopping motion with a hand. 'Standing by a tree outside my house. Then near the gym. Always bloody lurking.'

'Has she hassled you?'

'No. She's too far off for that.' She waggled a couple of fingers, 'a figure in the distance. Watching me. Between the bushes on the far side of the car park. Looking down from a footbridge as I drove beneath it.'

'So you're getting glimpses of her. What do the police say?'

'They're only interested in proper contact: phone calls, emails, knocking on my door. Stuff I can document.'

'She never actually approaches you?'

She looked at him again. 'The time on the footbridge, Joe. I saw her face properly for the first time...' Her fingers dug at her jacket pocket. Her hand came out and she flipped the lid on a packet of Marlboro Lights.

Joe took his Zippo from next to the ashtray and lit it for her. 'You saw her face?'

She dragged on the cigarette, eyes closed. 'All fucked up. Like someone had punched her in the mouth. Face was black with dirt and wisps of hair in these straggly little patches.'

'Didn't you say it looked like chemotherapy? Her hair?'

Mandy nodded. 'Yeah, kind of. I don't know. She could have hacked it off herself with a rusty blade. It was the look in her eyes. Daggers. Like I hate you. I really fucking hate you.'

Joe got to his feet and went over to the main window. He checked the street. A black Range Rover was parked directly below. 'That Wayne down there?'

'Yeah.'

'Has he not seen her?'

'No. But he is always driving.'

He directed his gaze across to the communal gardens which formed the centre of the square he lived on. There was a kids' play area in the nearest corner, a row of benches bordering it. The light was fading and the place was deserted. Dusk, he thought. The gates will be padlocked soon. At the very centre of the garden was an oval shaped expanse of grass. In the far corner was a large weeping willow tree. Someone was standing beneath its drooping branches. Joe dipped his chin and squinted. The figure was in shadow but seemed to be facing in his direction. It looked female.

'What have you seen?' Mandy's voice was strained.

'Not sure.' He crouched and slid a carry case out from under his desk. Inside it was his zoom-lens camera. 'I think there's a woman in the communal gardens.'

'No! For fucking real? Where?' She was beside him, fingers gripping the sill as if her legs might buckle. 'Where?'

He straightened back up, camera in his hands. 'Far end.

Under the willow tree in the corner.'

Her head moved like a hawk's and she scrutinised the area below.

Adjusting the lens, he sought out the mass of willow branches. Vertical tendrils of green crowded his vision and he zoomed back. A pair of legs came into view. 'It's a woman; she's wearing a skirt. Long.'

'She always wears a skirt! Christ, Joe. What about the rest of her?'

'She's beneath the branches. In fact, behind them, where they hang down. I can't make much out.'

Mandy was shifting from foot to foot. 'Can you get a photo? Will it come out?'

'No, not with this. It'd be rubbish.'

'Will you go out there, Joe? Please? Ask what the hell she – '

'Hang on. I saw a cigarette glow. She's...I think she's talking on a phone. Smoking a ciggy and chatting.'

'I've never seen her with a phone. She never has anything.'

'Well, this woman does. She's moving! She's coming out!'

They both watched as a smartly-dressed woman in her thirties emerged from the tree's shadow. A phone was slipped back in her bag and, after taking a final drag on her cigarette, she flipped the butt onto the grass and walked briskly for the nearest gate.

'Not her,' Mandy murmured, dragging on her own cigarette. 'That would have really freaked me out if she'd managed to follow me here.'

Joe continued to watch the woman's magnified image. She approached the terrace on the opposite side of the square. It was all apartments – young professionals, minus kids. Why the surreptitious call, he couldn't help speculating. What was she hiding? He was tempted to scan the building's windows with his camera. Work out which ones were hers. See what he could see.

'Joe?'

'Say again.' He lowered the camera.

'I wanted to ask a favour.'

'Go on.' He placed the camera on the desk and retook his seat.

She stayed where she was. He found her failure to also sit down annoying. The woman hadn't been out there. Mandy was being stressy and melodramatic over nothing. He wanted to tell her to drop her shoulders. Take a few deep breaths.

'Would you mind shadowing me for a bit? I'll let you know my schedule – it's strictly boring stuff, but if you can follow and keep a watch out for her. Get her on film, if you can.'

Shadow you for a bit, he thought. Did she mean the entire day? For how long? What about if he had work of his own lined up? 'You mean like, keep a watch out?'

'Yeah. She's piss-easy to spot. It would be simple.'

This was typical, he thought. Expecting him to drop everything for her. It didn't even sound like he was going to get any shots he could sell out of it. He waited for an offer of money. None came. Thinking quickly, he said, 'I've got a big assignment, Mands. I'm heading out the country – over to Nice.'

She seemed to wilt. 'What, like straight away?'

He nodded. 'Early tomorrow morning. I'm really sorry, the flights are booked and everything.'

She knelt at the coffee table, stubbed out her cigarette and settled back on her heels. 'Shit. She's a loony, Joe. I'm really scared she's building up to something horrible.'

'What about Wayne? He must have a camera on his phone. He takes you everywhere.'

'Wayne?' She made a popping sound through her lips. 'Fat bastard never gets out the car. Says it's not his job.'

Joe spread his hands, thinking the bloke had a point. Driver and unofficial photographer? That should cost extra. 'Let's talk when I get back. If you've spotted her again, I'm sure we could work something out.'

Her gratitude was sad to see. 'Cheers, Joe. You know I wouldn't ask for something like this if I wasn't – '

'Hey, don't sweat it. It'll be fine, honestly.'

She didn't look convinced. 'OK if I call while you're there?'

He grimaced. 'Mands, it'll be a round-the-clock job. My phone'll be off most of the time.'

She nodded. 'How long will you be gone for?'

'Two days.'

'So back on Friday?'

'Yup.'

'What time?'

'Late afternoon. It says on the e-ticket. Got it somewhere on my computer.' He flicked a hand towards his iMac in the corner.

'Late afternoon. Can I call once you're back?'

'Course.'

'OK, I'd better go.' As she stood, he glanced swiftly at his iMac. Now he'd have to go on the bloody internet and check the weather in Nice. And if it was hot, he'd have to fork out for a sunbed. Otherwise, she might suss out he'd never actually been away.

CHAPTER 13

His phone began to play *Buena Vista Social Club* once again. The device was on the coffee table, its screen just visible from his position on the sofa. Mandy again. He raised himself up on one elbow and checked the time. Was it six o'clock already? Time had flown.

He swung his legs off the sofa and sat with his head hanging down. His works were spread out before him on the coffee table. As he began to dismantle the syringe for cleaning and disinfecting, his phone started yet again. Christ, she was like a leech. He shook his head: he was meant to be feeding off her, not the other way round. He sucked air in sharply through his nose and grabbed the phone. 'Mandy! Hi.'

'I've been calling you.'

'Yeah – your messages have just started showing up. I've been on the plane. It got delayed.'

'Oh. But you're back now?'

'Yeah, heading for the train.'

'Can I come over in a bit?'

'What, tonight?'

'Yeah.'

'Well, I'm knackered Mands. Had about six hours' sleep since I last saw you.'

'I need to see you, Joe. Stuff's been going on.'

'Right,' he sighed. 'About eight, then?'

'Eight. See you then.'

He cut the call and flicked a V sign at the phone's blank screen. Fucking hell. She sounded totally wound up. He pictured her standing in the middle of the room, ranting on about her phantom stalker. He scratched at his forearm. And he'd forgotten to get a sun-bed session. His skin was its usual shade of white.

His buzzer went off at seven minutes to. He considered making her wait, claiming he'd been in the shower or something. It buzzed again and he trudged over and hit the button.

Seconds later, her double-knock sounded. He opened up, steeling himself for an emotional tidal wave. But she just stared at him from under the brim of an over-sized baseball cap. Her eyes seemed to have expanded in her head. He realised it was because of her face. It had shrunk in. The whole of her looked withered, older. Except her eyes. Fear made eyes go like that – a constant trickle of adrenaline putting them on permanent alert.

'Can I come in?'

He realised he was blocking the doorway. Stepping back, he said, 'What's been happening?'

Her movements were stiff as she checked the corridor and headed straight for the armchair, jamming a cigarette in her mouth as she sat. 'Got any vodka?'

He looked to the corner unit. 'The end of some rum. A bit of whisky.'

Her lighter clicked and as she exhaled the plume of smoke her head tipped back against the seat. 'No duty-free?'

He blinked. The flight. Shit. 'No. Prices are crap. I would have grabbed something in the supermarket. If I'd had time.'

'Whisky sounds good, cheers.'

He glugged some into a couple of shot glasses. He handed her one and it was gone in a single gulp. She dragged again on the cigarette, eyes closed.

'So,' he regarded her warily from the sofa. 'You want to tell me what's bothering you?'

Her eyelashes lifted and she glanced at him without turning her head. She looked back at her cigarette, spoke to the tip like it was a miniature microphone. 'I'm getting rid of these extensions.'

'Hey?' He realised every single strand was out of sight, squashed beneath her hat. 'Change your hair?'

'This all started happening after I had those extensions put in. They're causing it.'

Joe took a cigarette from his pack and lit it. He rubbed at his jaw line with the side of his thumb, smoke trailing up his sideburn like a climbing plant. 'How do you figure that?'

'It's because of them she hates me. I get them put in, photos of me are all over the place. She shows up within a day. And I know – from the look in her eyes – it's because of the hair.'

'I'm struggling here, Mands. To be honest with you. Nut-jobs are just obsessed about the whole celebrity thing. I don't think something like a new hair-style sets them off.'

'It has with her.'

Joe sipped his whisky with exaggerated slowness. He'd misjudged this. Didn't realise quite how freaked out she was getting. What a disaster. The hair was what had revived Mandy's profile in the media. She needed to keep the flow of shots up. Instagram. Twitter. Tumblr. He'd done a Nexis search for how many times the tabloid press had mentioned her: an increase of over two thousand percent. If she changed her look now, it would all vanish just as fast. 'Mands, you've not even had this new look a fortnight. It's too soon to change it.'

'I do not fucking care, all right? This woman...' Her fingers were trembling as she raised the cigarette to her lips.

'You've seen her again?'

'Seen her again? She's getting closer, Joe. Before, she'd

keep her distance, almost like she didn't want me to spot her. Not now. No fucking way now.'

He noticed that, in her agitation, traces of her West Country accent were slipping back. The burrs softened her words, robbing them of credibility. She sounded silly: a simple country girl. 'You said – before I went to Nice – she'd been up on a footbridge you drove under. Closer than that?'

'The other day?' She fed the end of the cigarette into the opening of the ashtray. 'I thought she was going to drop on my head.'

'Drop on you? Jump off the footbridge?'

'No. She was up a bloody tree on Wimbledon Common. I run there now and again.'

'Hang on. You're out jogging and she's waiting for you up a tree? Like an ambush?'

'Yes!' Mandy took another cigarette out and pointed it at him. 'An ambush, that's what it felt like.'

'But that's not stalking. Well, it is. But it's not following you.'

'How do you mean?'

'How often do you go on that run?'

'The Common? Maybe once a fortnight.'

'And you've been spotting her for how long?'

'This past week.'

'So, the last time you did that run was well before she first appeared? Before you even had the extensions put in?'

'Yeah.'

'So how could she have figured out you'd be – '

'Fuck knows. That's what's bugging me out. She just knows. I mean, the footbridge? What was she doing up there?'

'It's near your house?'

'Yes, but I was only taking the A24 because I'd rescheduled with Jerry, my personal trainer. He could only see me in the Virgin gym in Wimbledon. I'd never normally be driving along that road at that time.'

Joe tapped his fingers. 'Weird. She hasn't hacked your phone or something?'

'Hacked my phone? She's a fucking hill-billy wild woman. No way she even owns a phone.'

'This run. She's climbed into a tree? She's perched among the branches looking down at you?'

'And her hair – what's left of it – is fucked. Like she's got cancer and it's all come out in clumps. That's why I know this is all because of my hair. She's jealous, Joe. She is crazy bloody mad with jealousy. She wants what I've got so badly. She doesn't need to say anything, it's so obvious.'

'You don't know that, Mands. How old do you reckon she is?'

'Fifties?'

'Maybe you look like a daughter she lost. I don't know – maybe the shock of her daughter dying caused her hair to fall out. She might see you and it – '

'Why would she want to kill her daughter?'

'What?'

'I look like her daughter, yeah? She wants to kill me because of that?'

'You don't know she wants to kill you.'

'And you haven't seen her eyes. Daggers. Pure hatred.' She threw a tress of silvery hair over her shoulder. 'Actually, it was worse than hatred. I only caught her eye for a second, but...it was weird...intense. I stumbled. I actually stumbled.'

He kept quiet for a second. 'And the police?'

She hunched forward to light her cigarette. 'Bugger them. By the time they get their act together, she'll have stabbed me to death. The extensions are going and that's all there is to it.'

'What if you get rid of them and she still keeps showing up?'

Mandy shook her head, eyes back on the glowing tip of her cigarette. 'She won't. And even if she does? I've wasted a grand or two. It's worth it if it gets her out of my life.'

'I still think you should give it a bit more time.'

'No way. I'm booked in tomorrow. So, if you want another photo opp, be there for noon.

Joe reached forward to put his glass on the table. This was a nightmare. She was sacrificing everything because of some paranoid theory.

'Look at your arm. Didn't you see any sun down in Nice?'

He regarded his forearm, the glass in his hand poised just above the table's surface. The skin could have been made of that stuff for filling cracks in walls. 'Not stuck in a room overlooking a private pool.'

'Who was there?'

'Wife of some Formula One driver and an unidentified bloke. Curtains of the villa stayed closed. What'll you do for a new style?'

'I'm thinking crew cut, maybe even skinhead. It's worked for a few people before now. Jessy J for a start. Nothing Compares To You: the Irish woman who did that.'

Don't forget Britney Spears, thought Joe. She shaved hers off when she had her meltdown. Another thought occurred. Maybe this wouldn't be so bad. It would be like documenting a car crash as it actually happened. People loved that kind of hero to zero stuff. 'It'll certainly cause a stir.'

'Yeah. I could go with a military look. Desert boots and sleeveless vest. Might even get a tattoo on my arm.'

'Fucking hell, Mands, don't go too far. You're more traditional feminine. A look like that, they expect you to be mouthy, too.'

'How do you mean?'

'Spouting off about stuff. Third World issues. Women's rights. It's not you.'

She stayed silent. 'Yeah. I was going to have my lips re-done. Keep the babelicious look for my actual face. How about if I go feminine-sporty? Sort of a yoga style.

Trainers, leggings, vest and hoody. A softer colour palette.'

'Better.'

'Yeah, you're right.' She smiled tentatively. 'Thanks Joe.'

He sat back. 'Well, if you're going to do it, I'll be there to get it on film.'

'Can you contact that guy at *Snapped!* again? See what he'll offer for another exclusive.'

'Of course.'

'Cheers.' She posted her cigarette through the gap and gave the window an uncertain glance. She didn't seem very keen to leave. 'Hey,' she tried to smile as she unfolded her legs and stood. 'There's always the other option...'

'What's that?'

'You whisk me away to that bolt-hole of yours. No one would find me there. Not even this nutter.'

Joe pretended to give her suggestion some thought. If he knew she'd keep going on about the bloody bolt-hole, he'd never have dangled it before her.

'Christ,' she added, 'the thought of just kicking back there for a bit.' Her voice had grown languid and he looked across. She had her eyes closed again and he could imagine what was in her head; he'd painted the images for her enough times. A deserted beach, drift-wood burning on a fire, sweet smoke carrying across a rippling ocean, the sun slowly setting in the enormous sky.

He realised something then. She had no one. Any social circle from the village in Devon where she'd grown up had been left behind long ago – abandoned when she came to London. Of course, she knew people in the city – but only through what she did. And chasing fame for a living didn't lead you to pleasant, grounded people. God, he thought. I'm the closest thing she has to a friend. 'One day, Mands, we'll be sat there with a bottle of white wine, barbecuing fish I pulled from the sea minutes before.'

She reached out and closed her fingers on thin air. 'I'll keep that thought, thanks.' She put her hand in her pocket.

'Keep it nice and safe in here. Right,' she looked at the window once again. 'I know it's stupid, but do you mind keeping an eye out? Just until I'm in the car?'

'No problem. If she's down there, I'll open the window and chuck a plant pot on her head.'

She laughed. 'I'll see you tomorrow.'

She was on the pavement moments later. There was no sign of anyone as she hurried to the Range Rover parked on the corner. Just before jumping in the back, she looked up at him and gave a quick wave.

Her arm moved stiffly, and the brittleness about her was more obvious. Like she was something that could so easily crack and fall apart. As he raised a hand in response, he ran the fingers of his other hand across his camera.

Then he returned to the sofa, picked up his phone and selected a number. 'Nigel? It's Joe Sullivan. I've got another exclusive for you. Mandy Cost. Tomorrow, she's going to have another brand new look. No, honestly. What'll it be? Well, you know those extensions? The lot are coming out.'

CHAPTER 14

Father Thompson shifted uncomfortably on the wooden pew. They really were the most hideous things to sit on for any length of time. 'I think I know what you're going to say.'

Crowther turned his head, a questioning look on his face.

'Maggy Wallace – or her ghost – caused Mandy Cost's death.'

Nigel Crowther didn't respond for a second. 'I know, said out loud like that, it sounds absurd. But there...there are things that just can't be – I mean, the timings for a start.'

'How so?'

'Maggy Wallace was murdered almost three weeks ago. Mandy starts seeing this mystery person soon after. To start with, the person is just following her. But gradually getting nearer, building up to...'

Father Thompson cut in. 'And the person's appearance? That fits Maggy Wallace, too?'

Crowther nodded. 'It does.'

Father Thompson frowned. 'What? A chemotherapy patient? Dirt-smeared face and rags for clothes – I'm sorry, how does that resemble Maggy Wallace? She seemed to me a very proud woman who took good care of her appearance.'

'When she was alive.'

'Sorry?'

'He set fire to her, Gregory Lang did.'

'I beg your pardon?'

'After he strangled her.'

The priest's shoulders sagged. 'Go on.'

'First, he removed her hair – from as close to her scalp as he could. Then he took several books off her shelves. He ripped the pages out, scrunched them up and wedged them under the body. Wood from the basket, too. He did all this, then, once he thought it was ready, he lit the paper.'

Thompson was staring at the other man in shock. 'He told Joe Sullivan this? To his face?'

'Not to his face. Over the phone.'

'When?'

Crowther waved aside the question. 'I'll get to that. But Gregory Lang thought the fire would hold: he said her clothes were burning properly. But when what was left of her hair started crackling, the smell – it was too much. He got out.'

'And it didn't work.'

'No. The flames must have died down.'

Father Thompson looked away. He wanted reality to re-establish itself in his head. Solid, unalterable things. The heavily embroidered cloth draped over the altar. The reredos behind it. The walls. This was what formed the world. Not the shifting, sliding territory of what this man was telling him. He had to remember that. Had to keep a focus and not slip up. Not reveal in any way what he knew about Mandy.

The patch of sunlight had edged further across the crucifixion. Now Christ's upper torso and left arm were also swallowed by shadow. Soon, it would be more. The darkness would win. The priest had a sudden desire to not still be sitting here, listening to the man's words when it did.

A noise of metal grating on plastic caused him to look

down. Mrs Reynolds was working away at the underside of the vacuum. The light in the church was fading; he was surprised she could still see what she was doing. 'Mrs Reynolds, Rosemary – please, there's no need to do that now. I don't want you to injure yourself.'

'Nearly there, Father. Nearly there.'

Father Thompson was about to insist she go home when Nigel Crowther quietly spoke. 'You need to see the other photos.'

'Which other photos?'

'The ones taken by Joe Sullivan when Mandy Cost died. He captured everything, right from the moment she first appeared in the window.'

The priest hesitated. It felt like he was stumbling forward on marshy ground: every step he took, his feet sank deeper. Soon, he would be up to his thighs in this man's story. He glanced around. The shadows were gathering, blotting out the church's far corners. 'Well, this is hardly the place. Not in this light.'

To his side, the row of confessional booths stood dark and silent. He tried to shut out the memory as soon as it began to materialise. Mandy's whispered voice on the other side of the mesh screen. Her vulnerability was, to him, like a pheromone in the confined space. His gentle questions probing at her hopes and fears. The sound of her breathing making his pulse thud.

'Isn't there a room back there?' Crowther nodded to the shadowy space behind the altar. 'Where the choir hang their robes?'

'The vestry?'

'Yes, that's it. Has it got a table or something we could use?'

Father Thompson nodded. 'It has.'

'Perhaps we could...'

Grimacing as his legs straightened, the priest rose. 'This way.' He led the other man down the aisle. As they neared the altar, Mrs Reynolds looked up. She was on her knees, the cream-coloured hoover on its side before her. 'Here's the problem.'

There was a note of triumph in her voice as she lifted a hand. Something long and insubstantial trailed from her fingers. The priest was having trouble making it out.

'The brushes were totally clogged,' she announced. 'No wonder it wasn't picking much up.'

She was brandishing something that she'd cut from the machine's innards. Something that didn't quite keep up with the motion of her hand. He realised it was hair. A straggly great hank of matted human hair.

The tight pale curls of her perm seemed to glow in half-light as she admonished him with mock severity. 'Next time someone donates a hoover, check the rollers. This lot must have been collecting for months!'

Nigel Crowther was shrinking from the sight of it. The priest swallowed back his own feelings of revulsion. 'Oh gosh, that really has built up.'

Scissors still in her other hand, she laid the unkempt mane out on the carpet. A squaw with a victim's scalp. 'There's a little more on the back roller, but that's the worst of it.'

'Right. How very clever of you. So I imagine it will now work as it should.'

'I'm sure it will.'

'And there was me trying to check the dust bag.'

She tutted him in a good-natured way. 'That's practically empty. You get on Father, I'm sure this man won't keep you much longer.' Her eyes shifted to Nigel Crowther who stood mutely off to the side, attaché against his leg.

'Thank you Mrs Reynolds. Would you like me to wheel it back to...?' Thompson gestured towards the organ. At its side was tall, thin cupboard, its door wide open. Bottles of cleaning fluid lined the floor. Dusters and cloths were piled on the shelf above.

'No, no. I'm not quite done. I'll put it away when I am.

Would you like me to lock the front door with my key on my way out?'

The priest nodded. 'That would be very kind of you, thanks.' He turned to Crowther. 'Sadly, crime is becoming more and more of a problem; an entire collection box was ripped from its pedestal the previous year. Now we're more careful about leaving the church unattended. 'See you soon, Mrs Reynolds, see you soon.'

'Yes, good evening Father.' She bent forwards once more.

The priest beckoned to Crowther and they proceeded down the side of the altar to a small wooden door. Father Thompson twisted the metal ring half-way up and pushed the door open. After reaching inside, he flicked a switch. Warm orange light spilled across the cold stone at their feet. 'Welcome to my inner office,' he announced.

CHAPTER 15

Nigel Crowther dipped his chin: the doorway was low and he knew which would come off worse in a clash between the stone lintel and the top of his head. The vestry was a small room, made to feel smaller by what cluttered it: in the centre was a modestly sized wooden table with three mis-matched chairs. A hat stand was in the corner, two drab-looking coats suspended from the curling pegs at the top. Next to it was a sturdy-looking door that had a large key protruding from its lock.

'Where does that lead?'

Thompson followed the direction of the other man's stare. 'Into the church grounds. A path leads either across to the presbytery, where I live. Or, if you bear left, back to the main road.'

'So you keep it locked, then?'

Thompson studied the other man for a moment. 'Yes. Why?'

Crowther shrugged. 'I'm not comfortable in unfamiliar places. Knowing what's what, it just helps.' He continued to examine the room.

Attached to the wall beside the door was a wooden case. Its shelves were laden with books: some black, others red. Thinner pamphlets were piled on top. Directly beneath it was an open-topped wicker basket that contained an assortment of hats, knitted scarves, gloves, mittens and a couple of umbrellas. An old-fashioned desk was in the far corner, its fold-out front closed. Across the rest of that wall hung a row of white choir members' robes, their hems varying in length. On the other walls were several framed images: tranquil landscapes, a photo of a soaring Golden Eagle, an African child gratefully grasping a circular yellow biscuit.

A tapestry-like square of material hung from a horizontal wooden pole in the centre of the wall immediately to his left. Hand-embroidered, by the look of it. Crowther wondered if it was that which was making the room smell a little fusty. He guessed the item was a gift from an enthusiastic parishioner group. Probably elderly females. Judging by the adoring way the old dear outside had treated him, Father Ian Thompson was very popular with ladies of a certain age. Crowther could see why: the elderly man had a kind, intelligent face. Plus, he still sported a very impressive shock of hair.

The priest had started to swiftly gather in the pamphlets that covered the table. He half-turned his head. 'Please take a seat.'

Crowther was about to slide back a chair when he noticed another door. This one was in the corner of the room that had almost been behind him when he'd stepped inside. He immediately froze. 'What about that?'

Thompson glanced over. 'Oh – it's a toilet. I apologise now if you need it; the choir boys usually leave it in a shocking state. And Mrs Reynolds only cleans in here on a Friday.'

Crowther crossed the room and took a look inside. It was barely more than the size of a cupboard. The ancient-looking toilet had a wooden seat and heavy chain-link pull. But he wasn't interested in that: he was interested in the tiny window behind it. Through the frosted glass he could make out the silhouette of bars. He returned to the table and took his seat.

Thompson was looking at him with a dubious expression. 'Was it that bad?'

Crowther frowned.

'The toilet,' Thompson said. 'You didn't actually...'

'Oh, just looking. As I said, I like to know my surroundings.'

The priest searched for somewhere to put the pamphlets and decided on the floor. He managed to get within a foot of the carpet and then thought better of bending any lower. Instead, he let them drop. They connected with a dull thud. 'By the way, this bolt-hole the photographer alluded to. The one Mandy was so keen on. Does it actually exist?'

Crowther smiled a wry smile. 'Oh yes – it's real. Sullivan might not own it, but it's real. He booked a short-break there once.'

'Don't tell me: he's a frustrated wildlife photographer, too?'

'I think he's more interested in seascapes: the effects of natural light, stormy skies, that kind of thing. The place is on the east coast, not far from a town called Caister-on-Sea. You get some incredible dawns over there.'

The priest was frowning. 'Caister-on-Sea?' He lifted his eyes to the light above the table. 'Was there something in the news...?'

'The big wind turbine project? It's just along from it. The other side of a headland at the far end of the bay.'

'No, I was aware of that. Maybe something connected to it? A protest of sorts?'

Crowther looked blank.

'Never mind,' Thompson also sat, gaze settling on the attaché case.

Crowther immediately folded back the flap and extracted a green Perspex folder. Inside it, the priest could see a mass of photos. 'So,' Crowther announced, placing the leather case on the empty third chair. 'I mentioned that Joe took a whole slew of shots. Many of which we could never have possibly – '

'And I'd like you to know, I have no wish to see Mandy

Cost at the moment when she...as she lay dying. I still find it inconceivable someone could just stand there and take photographs.'

Crowther tipped his head. 'I understand. But isn't that how all the great images are captured? Nick Ut's one of the crying Vietnamese girl fleeing the napalm? Stuart Franklin's shot of the man blocking the tanks in Tiananmen Square? Dozens by Robert Capa: none would exist if those men had laid the camera aside at the crucial moment to try and help.'

'Those were moments in history – important ones.'

'And Mandy's death – '

Thompson cut in angrily. 'Please don't try and compare Joe Sullivan's motives with those photographers'. They weren't trying to make a quick buck out of another person's tragedy. If you ask me, your friend ranks with those people who took photographs of Princess Diana as she lay dying in that tunnel in Paris.' He flicked a hand. 'Now, what is it you want to show me?'

Looking chastened, Crowther reached into the plastic folder. 'Please, give me a moment.'

Thompson folded his arms and looked off to the side. In the periphery of his vision he could see Crowther shuffling his way through the collection like a card-cheat stacking the pack. The sharp clatter of plastic wheels encroached from beyond the door. Crowther shot a questioning glance at the priest.

'Mrs Reynolds,' he stated. The sound stopped and they heard a door being closed.

Crowther returned a dozen or so images to the folder. He placed another five or six face down at the side of the table. Then he scooped up the rest of the shots and laid them out in two neat rows. He gave a cough. 'OK, these at the top are the first Joe took. As you can see, there's very little going on initially.' His forefinger hovered above the end image. 'Mandy is just a blur really.'

Thompson looked down. Crowther was right; the shot

was a very plain, nondescript exterior of the second floor of a town house. Georgian, judging by the solid-looking brickwork around the window frames. It looked like a nice, quiet, tree-lined street that would cost an absolute fortune to live on. Behind the glass up on the second floor, a head and shoulders were only discernable. The hair extensions were gone, her slender neck just visible.

'So she's got out of the chair and is standing,' Crowther stated. 'In this next one, you can see her back is to the window. She's reacting to something on the far side of the room, I believe.'

Thompson's eyes moved to the second row of images. Mandy was now closer to the glass. She had begun to turn: you could see her shoulders had swivelled. But she was still looking across the room.

In the next, she was just inches from the glass. Her upper body was leaning forward: she was fleeing something. And her head had begun to turn in the direction of the window, revealing a mouth that was wide open.

In the photograph beside that, she was connecting with the window panes. Her hands weren't even raised. It appeared she'd run headlong at the glass. The pane at face level was splintering out; the expanding circle of cracks obscured her face.

Thompson found his eyes roving hungrily to the final image. It was like following a film in slow motion. Now the entire window frame was erupting. He was shocked at how she'd generated enough force to make the entire thing come apart like that. Glass was flying out in all directions and behind this silvery jigsaw suspended in the air, Mandy was partially visible. Her eyes were half-open, mouth still gaping. He wondered if she was even aware of the glass. Terror seemed to be in total control: why else wouldn't she close her eyes as her face hit the glass? 'Was there a scream?'

Crowther shook his head. 'Joe didn't remember one.

And none of the staff downstairs reported hearing one. Seems she just crashed straight through in a state of utter panic. In the next one, she's completely out – she didn't just fall against the glass and flop over the sill. She came through like a missile.'

Thompson looked at the pile of photographs that were face down at the edge of the table. Crowther had his hand on them, but didn't appear about to turn them over. 'You want to see them?'

Thompson gave him an encouraging nod.

'OK.'

Thompson thought he heard a trace of gloating in the man's voice. He checked his face, but Crowther only had his eyebrows raised slightly. 'I presume you're not going to show me her actually lying on the pavement?'

'No. Those ones went back in the folder.'

Thompson considered changing his mind; saying he'd seen enough. But the simple truth was, he hadn't. He wanted to see.

Crowther picked them up and created a third row. In the first, Mandy was in mid-air, top of her head now pointing at the camera. The first thing Thompson thought was how short her hair had been cut. She almost looked like an army recruit. A cloud of debris enveloped her and only now were her arms beginning to stretch out.

Sullivan was obviously having trouble reacting to events: the next two shots were of the shattered window frame. In the first, only Mandy's feet and ankles encroached into the bottom of the shot. In the next, she had vanished completely from view. Sullivan must have then lowered the camera: the final two shots were of Mandy on the pavement. The first image was blurred and her upper half was out of frame. In the next, she was at the picture's centre.

It reminded Thompson of photographs from war zones. That terrible spectacle of someone whose life had ended suddenly and violently in the street: clothes twisted, a hand palm up, one shoe hanging off.

Staring at the photo, Thompson became aware that Crowther was staring at him. He sat back and met the other man's eyes. 'After this, he closed in for a better view?'

Crowther lowered his head briefly in agreement.

The priest looked sadly at the folder with its stash of censored material. He sighed. 'Well, I'm glad you spared me them – and spared Mandy the ignominy of it, too.'

'Did you know her?'

The comment caught him totally off guard. Feeling a rush of blood to his face, the priest kept is gaze on the folder. 'Sorry?'

'Mandy. Did you know her?'

He took his time, careful to regain control before looking up. 'She visited fairly often – not for services. She'd just drop in when it suited her. But you are already aware of that.'

'Yes – it was the way you just spoke of her. Using her Christian name: as if she was, I don't know, more than someone who turned up every now and again.'

Thompson kept his face relaxed, but attentive. As a priest, hiding emotion was something he'd learned long ago. 'I was aware of who she was. Her public persona.'

Crowther appeared to be mulling the information over. 'Oh.'

The lack of response forced Thompson to say more. Cautiously, he said, 'Her appearance was...distinctive, for in a church. It wasn't long before news of who she was reached me: church goers, as much as anyone, like to gossip. Now, these photos – how do they indicate any kind of connection to Maggy Wallace?'

Crowther seemed to be looking through the priest, his thoughts entirely elsewhere. Then he blinked back to the present. 'A connection to Wallace?' His features sagged, worry and torment flooding his eyes once more. 'You have to look carefully. This one.' He slid an image out from the ranked group and placed it in the centre of the table, directly below the light. After licking his lips, he murmured in a dry voice, 'What can you see?'

Suspecting he was somehow being manipulated, the priest hesitated. He felt like a passerby, challenged by a street artist to name which cup was hiding the pea. It was an impossible game to win. 'What am I supposed to be looking at?'

Crowther whispered, 'The window. Not Mandy, the window.'

Thompson did as he was asked. The shot was the one of Mandy as she had gone through the glass. A miasma of pieces hung about her in the air. Her hands were coming up. Beside one shoulder, a section of wooden window frame was frozen in slow rotation. 'The window clearly has shattered,' Thompson stated.

'And behind the window. What can you see in the treatment room itself?'

Thompson looked more closely. So much movement was captured in the image, it was like looking from a speeding train and trying to make out details of the countryside through the trackside trees. But then the way his brain was processing the information altered; between the floating shards a face showed itself. A female face contorted by terrible fury. He glanced up to see Crowther's bloodshot eyes drilling into his.

'Is that not Mandy Wallace?' the other man quietly asked.

Thompson thought it was, but he couldn't admit that. 'It does appear someone was in the room.'

'It's her. Don't you agree it's her?'

I'm not agreeing to anything, Thompson thought. He reached for the pair of photos that followed it.

'She's not in those,' Crowther stated. Thompson studied the first: Mandy's feet were still in view. Though some smaller pieces of glass had yet to drop from sight, the view into the treatment room was fractionally clearer.

The room was empty. Same in the next shot. Thompson returned to the image of Mandy in mid-air. The face beyond the airborne debris was faint. Insubstantial. He lifted the photo, tilted it towards him then away, as if – like a kaleidoscope – the shards would shift to reveal the image beneath more clearly. He flipped it over and checked the other side. 'I think Joe Sullivan may have been playing about on his computer. Images, I gather, are very easy to doctor nowadays.'

Crowther shook his head. 'He had no idea, I'm certain. When I first spotted her face, I challenged him. He didn't know what I was talking about.'

Thompson tapped his fingers against the table. 'What amount of time is there between each shot?'

'Frames per second? In high speed mode, it's usually seven.'

'So, the person's face is in the centre of the room here. And in the next,' he pointed to the photo where Mandy's feet and ankles poked in at the bottom edge, 'it's not.' He clicked his fingers. 'Gone in an instant.'

Crowther said nothing.

'How about a staff member?' Thompson asked. 'Could that be who is visible?'

'I wondered that. The person who'd taken the extensions out had taken them downstairs – to have a few tangles removed by an assistant. Another staff member had just administered some injections; botox, to a few parts of Mandy's face. Some filler called restylane to her lips. They'd left her alone at that point, some quiet time while her face settled. And besides – that person has no hair, or very little. And she doesn't have the white tunic all salon staff wear.'

Thompson ran a finger down the edge of the photo. 'I assume staff reappeared upstairs pretty swiftly?'

'Yes.'

'And no one reported the presence of this person up there?'

'No.'

Thompson picked up the photo. There was no doubt whoever was in the room looked exactly like the reclusive woman who'd been murdered. 'Have you got that copy of your magazine? I'd like to see the photo of Maggy Wallace that is in it.'

Crowther went to lift his attaché, but stopped. 'It's on the pew where we were sitting. You left it out there.'

Thompson could remember placing it to one side. 'So I did.'

As he pushed his chair back and stood, a dull thud came from the main part of the church. Crowther immediately turned his head toward the door they'd come through. 'What was that?'

As the sound died away, Thompson looked down at the other man. His whole body was rigid. 'The main door at the front banging shut. I asked Mrs Reynolds to secure it on her way out.'

Crowther looked up at him, eyes bulging. 'That was the main door closing? You're sure?'

'I am. Back in a minute.' He walked across the room then looked over his shoulder. Crowther was hunched forward, hands clasped tightly in his lap. 'Sure you're OK?'

The other man gave a miserable nod.

Thompson opened the door and stepped into the main part of the church. It had grown noticeably darker and was now a degree or two colder. Two steps took him beyond the pool of yellow light spilling from the vestry.

Mrs Reynolds had left the spot light on above the main doors. From this distance, the narrow beam of light seemed ineffectual and small. Thompson checked the windows high above him. The sky outside lit them with a faint, greyish glow.

He started to walk and the only sound was his heels connecting with the stone floor. His footsteps were mighty in the dark and cavernous space. He usually relished the way it brought back one of his earliest childhood memories: story-time while sitting on his father's lap. This was how he imagined the giant's approach must have sounded to Jack where he lay hiding in the kitchen. Fe-fi-fo-fum. That delicious thrill of peril drawing closer.

But the evening's proceedings had soured his mood.

Instead, he walked with brisk purpose towards the shadow-filled rows of seats. The echo of his footsteps became more muted as he crossed the expanse of carpet before the altar. Then the noise grew hollow, offset with dull creaks as he strode across the wooden floorboards that ran up the main aisle.

At the third row from the front he stopped and looked along it. A square shape was just visible. The abandoned magazine.

In the vestry, Nigel Crowther listened to the priest's footsteps moving away. Rising swiftly from his seat, he crossed to the door in the far corner that led outside. He regarded the bolts at the top and bottom – neither were in place. Gripping the door's heavy handle, he tried to open it: the thing wouldn't budge. With a quick glance to the open door behind him, he clamped a finger and thumb on the key and twisted his wrist. It turned with surprising smoothness. He kept his grip on it and used his other hand to rotate the door handle. This time it opened. He could see asphalt and, beyond the narrow path, massed gravestones, the silhouettes of taller monuments showing against the fading sky. He pulled the door closed once more, turned the key the other way and retested the handle. Locked. He started to step back then changed his mind. His right hand lifted and he eased the upper bolt across. With a satisfied nod, he retook his seat.

Thompson picked the magazine off the smooth wood. The space between the two pews was narrow and he had to shuffle backwards, out onto the aisle. Turning to the altar, he saw Christ on the crucifix was now completely lost to shadow. From the street outside came the sharp bark of a motorbike; the rider taking advantage of a gap in the traffic to accelerate sharply.

Thompson continued to look at the figure. It was as if the effigy had slipped into murky water and was drifting from sight. The priest hadn't wanted to see Christ swallowed by darkness, but now he had. Trying to shrug off the feeling of disquiet it created, he turned his attention to the warm glow leaking out from the half-open door to the vestry. Suddenly, he wanted to be back there, even though he dreaded where the story of Nigel Crowther was leading.

CHAPTER 16

'Here we are,' Thompson announced, stepping into the vestry and pulling the door behind him closed.

Crowther was staring over. 'Was it the cleaner, that noise?'

Thompson nodded. 'Yes – she's taken herself home.'

'And she'll have locked the front door as she left?'

'Yes. We can leave by that one.' The priest pointed to the door in the far corner without actually looking at it. Placing the magazine on the table, he retook his seat. 'The story on Maggy – '

'Page sixteen,' Crowther cut in.

Thompson licked a forefinger and peeled corners back. 'Page sixteen.' He placed photograph of Maggy Wallace between them then positioned the shot of the breaking window beside it. 'I have to admit, that's odd. Whoever's in that photo does bear a strong resemblance – '

'Strong? The eyes, look at the eyes.'

Thompson didn't need to. 'So, this image is hard to explain. But I also should remind you, it was obtained – for a price – from a professional photographer. And I say again – '

'Joe didn't tamper with it. What I paid for the film was based solely on Mandy's death. If he knew about this face, he would have negotiated a separate fee.'

Thompson searched for an angle to explain what was before him. He was being asked to believe that Joe

Sullivan hadn't doctored the photo: that didn't mean the photo hadn't been doctored. It just meant someone else had done it. He looked at Nigel Crowther, a picture editor of a national magazine. Someone, no doubt, with years of experience in these matters. Was this some kind of elaborate joke on his part? 'I'm not clear as to your point. We have two tragic deaths – '

'Not two.'

Thompson's looked like the air had been sucked from his mouth. 'Not two?'

Crowther closed his eyes. 'Was your congregation comfortable with Mandy coming in here?'

The change in direction caused Thompson to flounder. 'Sorry?'

Crowther looked directly at him. 'You mentioned that it was through your congregation that you learned about Mandy. Were they happy about her wandering in? No disrespect, but half the time she dressed like she was on the game.'

Thompson sat back. 'She felt the need to visit. People aren't turned away – from this or any other church – on the basis of how they dress.'

'What's the average age of your regulars? Surely, something close to the lady who was fixing your vacuum? Sixties, seventies? People who dress respectably when they come to church. Am I wrong?'

The memory of an informal meeting was in Thompson's head. It had even involved Mrs Reynolds. Her and about ten other ladies who regularly came into the church. They'd claimed it was the sound Mandy's heels made on the floor; the jangle of her jewellery; the noise she made when chewing gum. It disturbed the peace and upset their thoughts. He could tell there was more to it than that. So, after they'd gone, he'd searched the internet for the name Mandy Cost. He'd found the sheer number of web pages that featured her astounding. It was scrolling through them that had led him to –

'I mean, I presume you realise how she first made a name for herself? The film the ex-boyfriend put online?'

Thompson placed his hands in his lap. Safely from sight, his fingers nervously sought each other out. His face felt hot and he didn't trust himself to speak.

'Sorry,' Crowther continued. 'I suppose you did. From the look on your face. That's what confused me: you've got someone in here who features in one of the most notorious sex tapes out there.' Crowther shrugged. 'I know it wasn't her who leaked it. But even so...'

'And surely you know it's not my job to judge someone on what may or may not have happened in the past. Now, it's getting late. You said something about there being another death – '

It was as if a draught had sought Crowther out. His shoulders shivered and he sucked in air through his nose. 'Yes – Gregory Lang. He committed suicide the day before yesterday.'

'The man who killed Maggy Wallace?'

'Yeah, him.' Crowther glanced nervously at the door leading out into the graveyard. 'He practically kicked the front doors of his local nick off their hinges, he was that keen to get inside.'

'When was this?'

'Six days ago.'

CHAPTER 17

'Help me! You've got to fucking help me!'

The front desk clerk looked up to see a man in his mid-twenties falling through the door. She had been in the job long enough to accurately assess most visitors in the time it took them to take three steps towards her screen. As the man regained his feet, face white and eyes practically popping out, she coolly appraised him. From the size of his pupils, she immediately concluded he was on something.

He twisted round to look back at the doors. 'Call your support!' he shouted over his shoulder.

She sat up straighter. He wasn't the victim of crime, not in the sense of a burglary or car theft. He wasn't here to report an incident he'd witnessed, either. She took in his jeans, new trainers, trendy jacket and cropped hair. His feet were wide apart, knees bent, as he cautiously approached the door to peer through the glass panels.

There were other people in the reception area. Ordinary folk there because of crimes they had suffered: they were dropping off insurance documents, waiting for follow-up interviews, arranging to view stolen items in the hope their missing possessions were among them. They didn't need to be caught up in a gang fight. Her hand hovered over the mushroom-shaped alarm button. 'What's the problem? Are you being pursued?'

Chest heaving, he leaned closer to the glass, head angling left and right. 'Ah fuck,' he whined. 'How can it be her? How can it?' He reached up to try and drawer the bolt across. 'Sir, please leave the door alone and answer my question. Are there people chasing you?'

'How does this thing work?' He continued to fumble with the mechanism.

Now unnerved by his behaviour, she pressed the button. 'Sir, tell me what's happening! Who's out there?'

'It won't work! What the fuck? She's dead. I know she's dead!' He tugged uselessly at the bolt's handle before realising that it needed to be rotated before it would slide across. He slammed it into place and, refusing to look away from the doors, took several steps backward. His heel made contact with the corner leg of the row of three seats directly in front of the doors. The ones no one chose, unless all those lining the walls had been taken. He sat down, shoulders rising and falling. 'Christ, this can't be, she was dead, you know she was dead. Oh Christ.'

Three male officers appeared from the rear part of the station. Shoulder-to-shoulder in the confined space behind the desk, they seemed like trapped animals, anxious to regain their freedom.

'What's up, Jenny?' an elderly sergeant called Adam Dunbar demanded.

The other two were leaning on the counter, eyes bouncing around the area beyond the Perspex screen. Faces stared back at them in worried silence.

'Not sure,' the clerk answered quietly. 'The guy sitting at the entrance? He just burst in saying he needed help. Like he was being chased. He bolted the door, ignoring my instructions not to. And started talking about someone who's died. Or someone he knew was dead. I think he's on something. Eyes are on stalks.'

'Do the buzzer, would you?' sergeant Dunbar asked, one hand on the can of CS spray attached to his utility belt.

She clicked the switch and all three of them filed swiftly out. They moved purposefully across to where the man was sitting.

'What's up, pal? Someone after you?' Sergeant Dunbar asked.

He nodded. 'Out there...I could see...oh, fuck.'

'You could see what?'

He shook his head.

'Who could you see?'

Now he said nothing.

'How many are out there? Two, three, more than three?'

He held up a single finger.

His answer visibly relaxed the trio. One officer went to the windows. 'Is this person chasing you armed?'

'No.'

The officer took a good look, glanced back at his colleagues and raised his eyebrows. 'I can't see anyone out there.'

The other two officers' attention started turning back to the man.

'You mentioned someone had died. Who?' demanded Sergeant Dunbar.

Gregory was about to speak, then stopped.

The sergeant leaned forward to look him in the eye. 'Who is dead? You said it was a female.'

He looked at the doors but said nothing.

'Are you using, son? What have you taken?'

His head shook: a refusal to reply.

'What's your name, son?'

'Greg.'

'Greg what?'

He was still looking over at the doors, but now more in confusion. 'Just Greg.'

'I'll have a surname, please.'

'Listen, I think I got a little mixed up, you know? I just want to sit here for a bit, get my head straight.'

'I asked for your surname.'

He shot the officer looming over him an irritated glance. 'I don't have to give you – '

'Are you on any form of medication?'

Greg started to shake his head as the officer at the door reached up to slide the bolt back.

'No! Don't open it!' Greg tried to stand but the other two officers shoved him back in his seat.

'Just calm it down.'

'Leave it!' Greg swept an arm out, connecting with the sergeant's thigh. 'She will – '

The arm he'd raised was grabbed and the elbow twisted back. Greg was yanked forwards, out of the seat and onto his knees.

'Get the fuck – '

His elbow was twisted higher and pain cut off his words as he went face down on the floor. The second officer had hold of his other arm. They brought his wrists together and a pair of cuffs appeared. Greg's torso bucked up and down, legs scissoring about on the shiny floor. 'Don't! Don't! No!'

The officer by the door unlocked it and pulled it open.

Greg was now shrieking, both officers straining to pin him down. The cuffs clicked and an officer's hand went from Greg's forearm to the back of his neck. Fingers clamped down hard.

'Stop the hysterics, son, and give us your name.'

Greg's voice was contorted and desperate. 'Stop, stop, stop.'

The officer by the door moved out on to the front step. He looked left and right then came back through the doors with a shrug. 'Nothing.'

Meanwhile, Greg's pockets were being turned inside out. First a phone, then a wallet was laid on the seat. The wallet was flicked open.

'Gregory Lang,' the sergeant announced. 'Run a check on that would you, Jenny?'

As the clerk behind the screen reached for her keyboard, she addressed the room. 'Sorry about this everyone. We'll have him removed very soon.'

The elderly couple in the corner were clutching each other's hands, the woman unable to look. A younger man near them had his phone held down near his thigh. Surreptitiously, he began scrolling through his menu to the video option.

Next, the sergeant held up a clear zip lock bag, white powder forming a triangular shaped dune in one corner.

'Oops,' the officer pressing Greg's head against the floor announced. 'Looks like you're under arrest, Gregory.'

Greg's body continued to twitch and jerk, but now his legs kicked with less force.

'What else have we got?' the sergeant asked, hands moving to Greg's jeans pockets. A set of keys came out.

'You live near here, Gregory?' the officer clamping his neck demanded, leaning forward so he could see Greg's face. 'You may as well – oh, Jesus.' His grip relaxed and he reached under Greg's head to lift it up. Foamy liquid flooded out from Greg's lips as his eyes rolled up to reveal their whites.

'Jenny!' the sergeant shouted. 'Duty doctor, now!'

CHAPTER 18

The duty doctor's sleeves were rolled up and his tie was tucked into the gap between the third and fourth buttons of his shirt. As he unwrapped the thick band from Greg's upper arm, a police officer watched impassively from the doorway of the medical room.

The doctor then removed the stethoscope from his ears. Strands of blond hair fell forward and he flicked them to one side with a sharp movement of his head. At twenty-three-years-old, he was younger than the majority of the people he was called in to check over. 'Your blood pressure and heart rate are up. Not significantly so, but elevated nonetheless. You said you haven't eaten much these last few days?'

Greg nodded. 'Crisps and that.'

'So it's no surprise, given the drugs and alcohol. Amphetamines especially.' He sat back and regarded Greg's sallow face. 'Got to start taking better care of yourself.'

Greg shuffled along the examination bed, turned sideways, lifted his legs up and leaned against the wall. His dirty socks were now almost touching the doctor's thighs. Greg raised his eyes to the narrow window near the ceiling. It looked to be sunny outside. Greg shivered.

'Drink your tea,' the doctor stated, gesturing at the vending machine cup on the side cabinet, 'the sugar will do you good.'

Eyes still fixed on the window, Greg leaned his head back. His eyes slowly closed and he thought once more about peering from the window of Maggy Wallace's cabin in the moments after he'd killed her. The trees had been shaking and bucking, but no storm had ever blown in. He also remembered checking the forest track; the leaves that littered it had been motionless. Completely still.

'Right.' The doctor placed his equipment back in his case, gave a nod to the waiting officer and stood.

'Hang on.'

He looked questioningly at Greg, whose eyes were reopening.

'Can I speak to you? Just us.'

The doctor glanced over at the officer. 'A couple of minutes?'

With a jangle of his keys, the officer said, 'The door stays open. I'll be just along the corridor.' He stepped outside and, making sure his footsteps were loud, took a few steps. Then, far more quietly, he moved back to the partially open door and listened.

Inside the medical room, the doctor had sat back down. 'What's bothering you?'

Greg studied the other man for a few moments. 'I saw this thing in a paper the other day. About exorcisms. This priest over in Italy, he's doing loads of them.'

'Yes, I gather the practice is far more common in Italy.'

'But they happen here, too? It's not just a foreign thing. The article said there are specially trained priests in this country that can do them.'

The doctor nodded. 'It certainly wouldn't surprise me.'

Greg picked at a blemish in the wall's smooth surface. 'Do you know how you'd get hold of one? How it works?'

'You mean contact a priest who can perform an exorcism?'

'Yeah.'

'As a doctor, I'm more interested in why you think that's necessary.'

Greg said nothing.

When the doctor turned his head, he could see a bulbous muscle pulsating at the hinge of Greg's jaw. Like a parasite stirring.

Greg's eyes moved to the half-open door. Then he whispered, 'I've been seeing a woman. I keep seeing her – but I know she's dead.'

'You know she's dead? How?'

'Because...I saw her. Stretched out. Dead.'

'You knew this woman?'

'No.'

'You mean, you saw a photo of her?'

'No. I saw her. You know, there.' He pointed at the floor. 'Right in front of me.'

'Where did you see her?'

'Just somewhere.'

'I mean in a nursing home, or a hospital?'

'No.'

The doctor frowned. 'In the road? A car accident?'

'No – in a building. She was lying on the floor in a building.'

'How did you know she was dead?'

'It was fucking obvious, all right?' Greg's fingers curled in and his eyes squeezed shut. He sighed. 'She was all fucked up – burnt. Quite badly burnt.'

'OK. Have you reported her whereabouts to the police?'

Greg's head shook.

'How long ago was this?'

'Five days.'

'And she's not there now?'

'I haven't been back. But – I did something stupid.'

'I don't understand.'

'While I was there,' Greg's hands moved towards each other, fingers and thumbs twisting.

The doctor watched their movement with an apprehensive look. 'What did you do?'

'I cut off her hair.'

'Sorry?'

'She had this really long hair. I know this place that pays cash for human hair. If it's long. So I cut hers off for the money.'

'I see.' The doctor looked profoundly dismayed. As if he might be in the wrong job. 'And now you're afraid this will count against you with the police?'

'Aye, I fucking know it will. Big time.'

'And you had contact with the body? I presume you must have in order to remove her hair.'

'Yeah, I lifted her head, turned it.'

'And this is why you're certain she couldn't have been alive.'

'Listen, she was fucking dead. No doubts. You don't lie there and let yourself be set on fire. She had. But now, I'm seeing her again. She's following me.'

'Is this woman young or old?'

'What does that matter?'

'I don't know.'

'Old. Granny age.'

'I see. How often have you been seeing her?'

'Seven times. Dusk, at first. But now during the day, too.'

'Are you at home when you see her? Just waking from sleep?'

'No – walking the streets, man. Outside. Always outside. She'll be standing under a tree. Or at the top of steps. Staring down at me.'

'Have you been sleeping much these past few days?'

'Hardly anything.'

'And consuming a lot of amphetamines?'

'Aye.'

'You obviously feel guilty that you removed her hair.'

'Feel like shit.'

'It's quite an intimate thing to have done, I imagine. You would have been close to her face. Looking at it.'

'I tried not to, but yeah.'

'You're agitated. You're tired. I think you need sleep, not an exorcist.'

'She's closing in on me. Before? When I ran in here? She was right behind me. I looked round and she was there, fingers outstretched. Like hooks.' He straightened an arm. 'That close, she was. And her eyes. Jesus, her eyes! I fucking ran, saw this place and was in.'

'Does she have a voice? Has she ever spoken to you?'

'No. Never says a word.'

'So you never hear her voice? For instance, when you can't see her, does she give you instructions or address you directly?'

'Never.'

'Let me have a word. See what the best options are.' He paused. 'The woman's body. Could you give me its location?'

Greg turned his head from side to side. 'No way.'

'She'll have family. People will be worrying. I really – '

'I'm not saying.'

'Why not? Keeping quiet like this, it's probably preying on your mind, adding to your sense of guilt.'

'Fuck her, all right? There's no helping her. Me, I'm the one who needs helping.'

The doctor stood. 'Please think about what I've said. No one deserves to be left like that. I think you agree. I think that's what's bothering you.'

Greg flicked a hand. 'Can you give me something? So I can sleep?'

'Let me have a chat.' He moved across the cell and leaned out the medical room. The officer was further down the corridor, studying the floor at his feet. 'We're all done in here.'

He looked up. 'All done you say?

The doctor nodded. 'For the time being.'

After the officer returned Gregory to his cell, he set off up the corridor with the duty doctor. In the large room at the end, the custody sergeant looked up from his desk.

CHAPTER 19

'What are your thoughts, Doctor?'

He placed his medical case on the floor. 'Well, he's not about to have a heart attack. Physically, he's OK, considering he's at the wrong end of a five-day-long binge. His mental state is a concern, though. The woman he mentioned: his sightings of her are very vivid.'

'The one who's meant to be dead?'

'Who he claims is dead, yes.'

'Did he say anything more about her?'

The doctor wondered how much he could reveal. What he had been told was in confidence, so he had to be careful. 'Not a lot. Just that she's dead. But he thinks she's stalking him.' He put his hands in his pockets. 'Paranoid, delusional, psychotic – I'm not quite sure. A proper psychiatric assessment from a mental health practitioner is my advice. He may well be better off in a secure unit for the time being.'

The custody sergeant twiddled his biro. That would involve several calls and a shed-load of form-filling. Sod that. 'Or he might be better after a decent kip?' he asked with an airy tone.

The doctor pursed his lips. 'It certainly wouldn't do him any harm. But I think his problems go further than that.'

'Good,' the officer said, ignoring the doctor's second point. 'He can get his sleep at home. We'll be needing his cell this evening for the usual traffic.'

'You aren't going to keep him in? the doctor asked.

'On what grounds? Running in and locking our front door? Possession of a pinch of speed? That's a caution, at most. Though, to be honest, we're not really bothering when the amount's that small.'

'The woman he believes is dead. Doesn't...shouldn't that be looked into? I mean, if there's a body somewhere – '

'Is there a body? He said nothing to us.'

The doctor thought through his reply. 'I think it might be worth asking him how he's so sure this woman is dead.'

The custody sergeant held his palms out. 'He'll tell us nothing. You know that. I've checked the system. Gregory Lang has been cautioned on numerous occasions for drug-related offences. He's a low end dealer at most, probably consumes far more than he sells.'

The doctor picked his case up. 'Fine. So it's back out on the streets, then.'

'Unless you'd care to start setting things in motion – for that bed on a secure unit you mentioned.'

'I'm satisfied he's stable, physically. I'll email my report.'

'Thanks, Doctor. See you about.'

Once they were alone, the custody sergeant turned to his colleague. 'Right, No Further Action it is. Care to kick his skinny arse out of here?'

The officer smirked. 'I ear-wigged the chit-chat. The doctor and him.' He nodded in the direction of the medical room. 'When I was out in the corridor.'

The custody sergeant lifted his chin. 'Yeah? What was said?'

'The woman he thinks is following him? Our man was claiming to have seen her dead body lying in a building somewhere. This woman had long hair, so he cut it off.'

'You what?'

'To sell it on to someone. Does that happen?'

'You mean, will people pay for human hair?'

'Yeah.'

He shrugged. 'People will pay for anything, if you ask me. No matter how weird the stuff, there's always some sick fucker somewhere into collecting it. What else?'

'He said the woman's body was badly burned – that's why he knew she was dead.'

'All of her was burned?'

'Presumably.'

'All, except her lovely long hair. That was fine, was it? He's full of shit.'

'What I thought. He was also trying to tap up the doctor for pills.'

The custody sergeant gave a knowing nod. 'That's what his game is. Well, he's not scoring in here. He can go back to his usual haunts for that.'

His colleague grinned. 'I'll fetch his stuff.'

Twenty minutes later, the door to Gregory Lang's cell opened once more.

'That's you done,' the officer who'd accompanied the doctor earlier announced, 'all your possessions are waiting for you on the front counter. Home time.'

Greg was in the corner, back against the wall. His head swivelled round and he blinked.

The officer clapped his hands. 'Action stations! Get your arse in gear!'

Greg licked his lips. 'Where am I going?'

'Out. Home. Wherever it is you live.'

'Outside?' Greg raised his knees up and clasped his arms. 'Where's that doctor? He was getting me some medication.'

'Long gone, my friend. Better things to do than provide you with pills.'

'He's gone?'

'Correct. Now, up.'

'But he said he was finding some stuff out for me.'

'Did he now? Well, maybe he'll give you a call later. Now, up.'

Greg shook his head.

The officer gestured at the door. 'Come on, you're not staying here.'

'I'm not going.'

The officer placed his hands on his hips. 'I didn't quite catch that.'

'I don't want to go.' He looked at the window: the glow now spilling through was orange. Outside, the street lighting had come on.

The officer raised an eyebrow. 'This isn't a hotel: shift your arse.'

Greg tilted his head away from the officer and looked directly at the wall. 'I want to speak with that doctor. He...he didn't say I was being released.'

'Enough of this. Toddle along to accident and emergency, if you want a doctor. On your feet. Now.'

'Leave me alone.'

'I'll leave you alone when you're walking out the front door of this place.'

Greg gripped his legs tighter and stayed silent.

The officer walked across the narrow cell. 'Stop this shit now or things'll get nasty. Your choice.'

Greg turned his head back. Eyes on the officer, he sat up straight, swallowed, then smashed the back of his skull against the smooth concrete. Eyes glazing over, he wrenched his head sharply to the side and cracked his nose and face into the adjacent wall. A line of red wormed its way out of one nostril and over his lips and chin. Fat spots started appearing on his chest.

The officer was roaring for assistance as Greg drunkenly tried to connect with the wall a third time.

CHAPTER 20

Father Ian Thompson got out of his chair. He needed to gather his thoughts. He needed to be free of the other man's stare. It had a forlorn intensity. It was wretched and it was making the priest feel the same way. Infecting him.

There was another reason he needed to put some space between him and the other man. Nigel Crowther was beginning to smell. Perhaps the acrid body odour had always been there – but in the close confines of the vestry it was magnified. The priest couldn't stop it encroaching into his nostrils. He'd tried to sit back but it was like a miasma, corrupting the air.

The priest wandered over to the wicker basket. He reached down and righted a rolled-up umbrella that had toppled to the side. He pulled a glove clear of the pile, rummaged for the one that matched. The unfolding events were beginning to truly unsettle him. He spoke with his back to the other man. 'What happened next?'

'The duty doctor was called back. Lang had suffered concussion. So now he was disoriented as well as extremely agitated. He ended up being sectioned and was taken to the Mental Health Unit at The Royal Glasgow Hospital. It was in there that he – you know – died.'

Thompson didn't know. He could sense gaps: spaces between what had happened and what Crowther was saying. He knew there were connections; he just couldn't see them. Or they were being obscured. 'Forgive me, I'm having trouble...' he pinched the bridge of his nose, eyes squeezed shut. 'For example, how did you get involved? Something takes place up in Scotland, hundreds of miles away, and you're immediately aware of it.' He looked at the wall, blinking. 'Gregory Lang's arrest, for example. There'd been no official announcement, or had there?'

'Not that I know of.'

Thompson wandered back to the table. Undecided whether to sit back down, he hovered beside his chair, one hand resting on the back support. 'So how did you get on to it so quickly? Your photographer friend: he's spoken to, not only the custody sergeant, but Gregory Lang himself. How?'

Crowther picked at the corner of the table with a thumbnail. 'Once I saw Maggy Wallace in that photo of Mandy going through that window, I rang Joe. I was extremely angry, at first. I thought it was a trick – like you. I asked Joe what the hell he was playing at. He didn't have a clue, genuinely didn't. So I asked him to my office. After he'd looked at the photo, we sat there for several minutes. Neither of us spoke. Joe wondered if I was winding him up. Anyway, after a bit, he said – almost jokingly – to suppose it was Maggy Wallace's hair that had ended up at the salon in London. If it was, who had supplied it?'

Thompson dragged the seat well back from the table and sat. It seemed, from this distance, he was safe from the other man's reek. 'And from that, you assumed the extensions Mandy Cost had fitted were Maggy Wallace's hair?'

'It was just a theory, the best we could come up with. So we called the salon and they gave us Gregory Lang's details. Then we set about trying to locate him. A police contact we use at the magazine was able to tell us he had recently been arrested up in Scotland. The records showed he'd been quickly released into the care of The Royal Glasgow's Mental Health Unit.'

Thompson nodded in understanding. Crowther and the

photographer might not be actual reporters, but they could sniff a good story. 'So Joe Sullivan jumps on his motorbike and roars off up to Scotland?'

'He's at the police station that evening. He catches the custody sergeant coming off duty and gets the full account of Gregory Lang's arrest.'

'Just like that? An officer involved in an ongoing investigation happily chats away to – '

'Joe paid him,' Crowther stated matter-of-factly. 'It's how half the stories you read make the papers.'

Thompson crossed his arms. The man's flippant attitude rankled. 'So that's how you got the policeman's side of the story. And Gregory Lang's? I'd love to know how your photographer friend spoke to him. After all, was he not – at this particular point – sectioned for his own safety?'

Crowther' face reddened as he murmured, 'Yes. Yes, he was.'

'And?'

The other man's eyes slid across the table. They crept up to Thompson's chest, darted to make contact with his face, then dropped again. 'Joe decided, after we talked, that...we had his number, you see. The salon gave it to us.'

'You had the number for his mobile, yes.'

Crowther shrugged. 'It...it was just a case of Joe trying it. To see if Gregory answered.'

'Even though he's in a secure unit?'

'Yes, but he's not in a straitjacket, not locked in a padded room. He had access to his phone.'

'And then what? Gregory divulges that he'd murdered Maggy Wallace, hacked off her hair, attempted to burn the body, and sent her hair to a salon in London? All this to an utter stranger who happens to call him?'

'Well, no. Joe needed to put him at ease first. Then they talked.'

Thompson dipped his chin while continuing to stare Crowther directly in the face. 'I don't know exactly what you want from me. But I'll tell you this: I cannot help you if you're being anything less than honest. I need the truth. Not just the bits and pieces you find it convenient to mention. If you're not prepared to do that, leave right now. Which will it be?'

Crowther swallowed. He looked queasy. There was a sheen of sweat on his face and Thompson's nostrils were soured by a fresh wave of body odour.

'It was Joe who suggested doing what he did. Not me.'

Thompson leaned back and waited.

Crowther took in a deep breath. 'What you just said to me...that's essentially what Joe said to Gregory Lang.'

'What was?'

'That if Gregory wanted help, he'd have to tell everything. The lot. That's what Joe said.'

'I'm having trouble making sense of this. Why would Gregory feel obliged to tell Joe a single thing?'

'Because...' Crowther went to pick at the corner of the table again. He changed his mind and his hand flopped loosely into his lap. 'Because of who Gregory Lang thought he was. Joe knew from the custody sergeant that Gregory had wanted an...someone that could, that could...' He cleared his throat. 'Do exorcisms.'

The anger Thompson felt was like a wave of compressed air. It surged through his chest and down his arms. His fingertips tingled. 'The photographer pretended to be an ordained priest?'

Crowther kept looking down as he nodded.

Thompson counted to ten, but it didn't do much good. 'It's hard to imagine a more despicable trick to play. Particularly on someone as unstable as Gregory Lang. Tell me what this friend of yours said to him.'

'He's not my...' Crowther's sentence dried up. He looked miserable as he began to speak. 'He got through to Gregory and said that the duty doctor from Crofthill Road police station had contacted the Bishop of Glasgow's office, that he'd, you know, asked about locating a priest who could perform an exorcism. I'm not proud about this, it's...it's making me feel...' he cleared his throat again, pressing a palm against his sternum.

'Just tell me,' Thompson said flatly.

'Joe said the offices of the Bishop of Glasgow had rung the Archdiocese of Westminster, that he was based in the Archbishop's office there, that he was officially sanctioned by the Vatican to perform exorcisms in Britain.'

'That's not how it works.'

Crowther gave a half-shrug. 'We just looked at a page on Wikipedia.'

'We? I thought you said this was all Joe Sullivan's doing?'

Crowther' face flushed again. 'I...I did the research for him. I was at my computer, so it was easier for me.'

Thompson's voice was cold. 'Carry on.'

Crowther looked like he might retch at any second. 'Joe explained the call was confidential. He said that, to assess whether an exorcism was warranted, Gregory would have to confess everything – all his sins. Concealing anything would be sacrilegious.'

'And Gregory agreed because he was terrified. I imagine he was begging for help.'

Crowther nodded. 'Joe got the full story from him. Every little bit.'

'And then? How did Joe leave things with Gregory Lang?'

'Gregory was convinced he'd been seeing her again.'

'Who?'

'Maggy Wallace.'

'In the Mental Health Unit?'

'Outside it. Through the windows that faced towards this row of trees. I think Gregory said fir trees. Anyway, he thought Maggy was among the branches looking in at him.'

Being spied on. A typical belief, Thompson thought, of those suffering paranoid delusions. 'And your friend's advice? What help did he offer someone going through what Gregory Lang was going through?'

'I think he just said to stay strong, have faith, and that he'd be there as soon as – '

'Oh for pity's sake! The man believed help was coming? I cannot believe you'd do something so irresponsible. So disgraceful. In fact, so bloody cruel.'

Crowther glanced up for a second. 'Yeah, well, like I said – it's not something that makes me feel – '

'When was Gregory expecting this visit?'

'First thing the next day.'

'And when did he commit suicide?'

'That evening.'

'That evening? How?'

'It's sketchy. Joe got a call from the custody sergeant the next morning. The guy was crapping himself – the detectives investigating the murder of Maggy Wallace had been in touch: they now had Gregory Lang as their prime suspect.'

'How did they make the connection?'

'The officer who'd been eavesdropping? When Gregory Lang was talking to the duty doctor? He logged that information on the police computer system; their national database. Just in case a badly burned body ever showed up.'

'And that information was somehow found?' Thompson asked, crossing his legs and leaning well back.

'Yes – Maggy's body had been discovered within days of Gregory Lang killing her. A murder investigation was opened and details from the crime scene were entered on the system. When that information matched with what had been logged by the officer at Crofthill Road station, a flag was triggered with the team investigating Maggy's murder. Locally, news was also spreading of the crime. A bus driver came forward and reported dropping off a lone male on the road near Maggy's cabin. When the murder team showed him the mug shot from Gregory Lang's records, the bus driver said it was the same man. They were preparing to question Gregory – they were actually about to set off to the Mental Health Unit – when news came through that he was dead.'

'You didn't say how he died.'

'According to the custody sergeant, Gregory asked to visit the chapel on the Mental Health Unit the previous evening. To pray.'

'Let me guess,' Thompson said. He knew contempt was spilling into his words, but he didn't care. 'Could that have been right after your photographer friend spoke to Gregory Lang?'

Crowther shifted in his seat, still looking down. 'The chapel's on the top floor. Domed glass roof in the middle, lots of light. Gregory had been in there for around two hours – then there's a great big crash. Alarms go off and a staff member rushes in. Gregory had forced open the emergency exit door and jumped over the railings.'

'No wonder you feel so guilty,' Thompson remarked. 'You should do.'

Crowther raised his face, eyes glistening. 'Thing is, he didn't want to be outside, did he? He wanted to be inside. Somewhere safe. You'd think the Mental Health Unit would have been enough.'

'The man was deeply disturbed! And you validated his fears – made them real – by leading him to believe an exorcism was – '

'I think it was her.'

'Sorry?'

'I think Maggy Wallace appeared in that chapel. The domed roof? I've seen images. It has vent things – gaps that open up.'

'I'm not going to respond to that.'

'The custody officer also mentioned to Joe some details about the crime scene at Maggy's house.'

'What kind of details?'

'Maggy Wallace was interested in pagan things: phases

of the moon, herbs, that kind of stuff.'

'That doesn't make her a witch. I know that's what you're insinuating.'

'Gregory Lang described to Joe how, before dying, Maggy Wallace grabbed hold of something. Remember? She was clutching something and mumbling as she died.'

The priest gave a resigned nod.

'The custody sergeant at the station had seen the crime scene photographs. He'd seen what it was she'd been clutching. He described it to me and it didn't take me long to find pictures of similar objects.'

Thompson lifted a hand and flicked his fingers. 'I'm not going to accept Maggy Wallace was a witch – much less in league with dark forces or whatever you will – because she owned some kind of amulet and had an interest in homeopathy. Give in to those kind of thoughts and you'll be the one who ends up seriously disturbed, I'm sorry.'

'It wasn't an amulet. Gregory Lang thought it was a letter opener; something she had wanted to use as a weapon. But it was something else: an athame. Do you know what that is?'

Thompson studied his hands. 'No.'

'It's a ceremonial knife witches use to summon magical powers.'

'Not just a craft knife? Or a harmless letter opener as Gregory thought?'

'Its handle was black. There were things engraved on it – symbols. A pentagram was at the centre. And when forensics were dusting for prints, they noticed the powder was being attracted to the blade. It had been magnetised. The blades of athames are always magnetised to give them extra potency.'

Thompson tipped his head back and regarded the light above them. 'Well, everyone else dismissed her as a witch so you're not alone.'

Crowther sat forward, elbows on his knees. 'I'm

not...this isn't a way to make her out as evil. I don't believe she was. She was solitary by nature, but her body didn't lie there for weeks undiscovered. It was found because people kept an eye out for her.'

Thompson lowered his gaze. 'Who did find her body?'

'A young lad from the village. She helped him once. He was out in the woods playing with friends and got badly injured.'

'Joe Sullivan has also spoken to him, I take it?'

Crowther nodded in agreement. 'After Glasgow, Joe travelled straight to where Maggy Wallace lived.'

'And this lad. Does he have a name?'

'Russ. Russ Cowan.'

CHAPTER 21

'Will these be long enough, Russ?'

'I reckon. Let's lay one on the ground underneath. We'll be able to see that way.'

The three boys were standing beside a huge cedar. Its trunk divided very low down, providing an easy initial step up. A second split in the right-hand trunk gave access to the tree's lower branches. They fanned out at almost horizontal angles. The V-shaped gap between two of the thickest boughs was what interested the trio.

'Come on then.' Russ turned to the untidy pile of planks. They'd removed them from behind a unit on the small industrial estate at the edge of town. The business that had occupied the squat building had been something to do with garden furniture. But, like many of the other companies, it had gone bust. Now the most common sign on the front of the units said the same thing: To Let.

Russ hitched up his tracksuit bottoms before squatting down. He was almost eleven-years-old and the smallest of the group. Short black hair, pale skin and eyes that were bright blue. 'Jim, come on.'

A heavy-set boy with ginger hair and round cheeks kissed by freckles moved to the other end of the plank.

'Shall I get the hammer?'

The question came from the third boy. Andrew was Jim's younger brother. Aged nine, he was just beginning to develop a belly like Jim's. Russ had noticed, with a pang of envy, that the pair of them always had crisps in their packed lunches. And, when they got in from school, their mum directed them straight to the snack box. Russ loved it when they invited him in: the choice was brilliant. Wagon wheels, Penguins, teacakes, caramel wafers. It was a routine that required no words. Lid off, delve about, head to the front room, telly on until she called them through for tea.

But Russ didn't like sitting around for too long. It made his blood go syrupy in his veins and his lungs felt like they were losing their ability to work. He'd fight the sensation by sucking in mouthfuls of air and twitching his legs.

'They're kicking again,' Jim would announce, eyes leaving the screen for a moment. 'Restless Russ.'

'Let's do something.'

The comment used to draw interest from Jim. He used to sit up and ask, 'What?'

'Kick a football around? See who's down at the rec? Head for the woods?' But, lately, Jim's response was just a wrinkling of the nose. Since their dad had got a smart TV that let you go on the internet, Russ noticed the two brothers spent more and more time slumped in front of it. YouTube videos, mostly.

Russ had spotted the planks a few days before, when he'd taken the long way home from school. The next day, he'd mentioned them to Jim along with his idea for a tree house. To his delight, Jim's eyes had regained their sparkle. It was like a spell had fallen away.

'A tree house? Yeah! Up in the woods?'

Their plans had grown rapidly grander. Not just a platform between two branches; they'd give it a roof, too. Behind another unit, they'd found a roll of thick black plastic. The roof could be waterproof! There was a rug for sale in one of the charity shops, the one along from The Castle. The lady was happy with two quid for it. They could bring food out with them, have picnics in there. Russ suggested going to the second-hand bookshop. They could get a load of cheap comics and annuals from the kids' section for next to nothing. Have stuff to browse through. After all, there was no internet signal out in the woods. No electricity, either.

So began the long process of ferrying the materials out to the tree they'd chosen. Things became a lot easier when they borrowed a wheel barrow from the man who lived next door to Russ. But it was still a long slog along the track that led up through the woods.

'Shall I get the hammer?' Andrew asked again.

Russ looked at the Farmfoods carrier bag. The end of the hammer and the handle of a saw were poking out. Filling the bottom was a load of huge nails they'd sneaked from the shed in Russ' back garden. His dad had left a couple of years back, so they wouldn't be missed. 'Let's line up a few of these planks first, hey Andy?'

He and Jim lifted the longest plank and carried it close to the tree. The two boughs they were targeting were about seven feet off the ground: not too low, not too high. Russ was already wondering about a rope ladder. But the one he'd seen on eBay cost way too much.

He bent his head back to assess whether, once lifted into the tree, it would stretch between the two branches. 'About here?'

Jim was studying the distance, too. 'Back a bit more.'

The plank was laid on the layer of pine-needles that covered the forest floor. They returned to the pile and selected the next longest. This was laid alongside the first, on the side nearer to the tree's trunk. The next longest was laid alongside that. By repeating the process, they formed a wedge-shaped platform of wood that, once in position, would come to within stepping distance of the trunk.

'You know what?' Jim said with a grin. 'Once we nail them in place, we could sleep up there. There'll be room enough.'

Russ' eyes widened. He immediately pictured being up there in the dark. They could bring candles in empty jam jars. Snuggle down in sleeping bags, blankets over the top, listening to owls hooting. Night creatures would pass by beneath and they could catch them with torch beams, watch as they raced for cover. It would be brilliant. So much better than at home, where he was stuck on his own so much of the time.

'Can I get the hammer?' Andrew asked.

'You get the hammer,' Jim said, rolling his eyes at Russ. 'How shall we do this?'

Russ thought for a second. 'What if I climb up? You're the strongest, so you stand a plank up and lift it to me. I drag it across the branch and slide it across to the other one.'

'I can be on the other branch,' Andrew cut in, striding towards them, the hammer swinging from one hand. 'To grab the end of it as soon as it comes within reach.'

'Yeah,' Russ nodded. 'And you can hold it in place while I nail my end down.'

'Let's do it,' Jim said. 'This is going to be so good.'

Russ took the hammer off Andrew then went over to the Farmfoods bag and shoved a load of nails into the deep pocket of his tracksuit bottoms. At the base of the tree, he stuck the handle of the hammer into his waistband before clambering swiftly up. Once on the correct bough he crawled out along it.

Below him, Jim watched with an eager expression. 'Whoa!'

Russ came to a halt and looked down. He was directly above the largest plank. Andrew had climbed up after Russ and was already out on his bough, straddling it. The two of them exchanged a quick smile as Jim stood the plank upright. Russ sank down low on his knees and, by reaching down, could almost touch it. 'Bring her up!'

Jim half-squatted, grasped each side of the plank and straightened his legs. It rose enough for Russ to grab the end. As Jim fed it up through his hands, Russ guided it across the branch he was sitting on. Soon it was spanning it like a see-saw, the far end inches from Andrew's outstretched fingers.

Russ slid it a little further out. Soon it was taking all his strength to keep the far end from dipping too low. Just as he was about to lose control, Andrew's fingers made contact.

'Got it!'

The youngest boy pulled the end onto his branch. They'd done it. The largest, heaviest plank was in place. From now it would only get easier. Russ slid the hammer out of his waistband and took a nail from his pocket. They were five inchers, silver, and with a nice sharp point.

Still kneeling on the branch, Russ hammered a nail in. The harsh noise of metal hitting metal rang through the quiet woodland.

Andrew giggled. 'Making my branch shiver. It feels funny.'

Russ felt the nail's resistance to each blow lessen and guessed the point of it was now passing into the softer wood of the branch itself. He kept hammering until it was fully in.

Jim's voice came from below. 'How does it feel?'

Russ placed the hammer on the branch, grasped the plank's end and alternated the downward pressure of each hand. The plank's sides lifted and fell. 'A couple more, to fix it properly.'

He knocked in two more nails until they were flush with the plank's surface. 'That's not going to shift. Andrew? Keep your weight on that end, I'm coming over.' Pushing the hammer before him, Russ started crawling across the length of wood. It was too narrow for one knee to pass the other, and he was forced to swing each leg out slightly. Half-way across, he wobbled. Andrew and Jim looked on in open-mouthed silence. Russ waited until he was steady and carried on. A metre later, Andrew was able to reach out and pluck the hammer from the plank. Russ closed the remaining distance, and when he made it onto

Andrew's branch, the other two let out a cheer.

'Crawling the plank,' Jim stated, face turned upwards. 'The new thing on pirate ships.'

Russ laughed as he put the first nail in position. Andrew handed him the hammer. Minutes later, the heads of three nails studded the plank's end. Russ tried waggling it. 'Solid as a rock,' he announced, inserting the hammer's handle into his waistband and standing up. 'I'll walk it this time.'

Arms held out at either side, he stepped nimbly across it to the other bough. Andrew gave an appreciative clap. 'I want to try.'

'Wait until we've got the second one in place,' Russ replied, kneeling down. 'It'll be twice as wide then.'

'He's right,' Jim said in a strained voice, lifting the next plank up.

Russ took its end and guided it across the gap. This time, Andrew reached out and was able to take hold of his end slightly sooner. But when Russ tried to lay his end flat, something pushed back. He craned his neck to see down the side of the bough. A slender side branch jutted up. 'Jim, I need the saw.'

'OK, boss.' He retrieved it from the plastic bag. Holding it by the end of the blade, he lifted the handle to Russ' outstretched fingers. 'Got it?'

Lying flat against the branch, Russ strained his arm down. 'No, I'm too high. Is the twine in the bag?'

Jim trudged back. 'Yes.'

'Tie the end of it round a nail. Then chuck the nail to me. We can hoist the saw up that way.'

Jim tapped his forefinger against his temple. 'That's brains for you.'

The nail rose up in the air, a strand of green twine trailing behind it. Russ had to lean back to stop it hitting him in the face. It caught in the branches above him. A tug on the string freed it.

Below, Jim was tying the other end of it round the

saw's handle. 'OK.'

Russ pulled the string up and the saw rose smoothly above Jim's head and into the canopy.

'Are we a team, or what?' Andrew stated, slapping his palm against the plank.

Russ laid the tool across the secure plank and undid Jim's knot. The obstructive branch was only a few centimetres thick. If he cut through it near the main branch, the remaining stub wouldn't be a problem.

He began to saw, but the side branch was thin: it kept bowing and the teeth of the blade wouldn't bite. Russ gripped it with his free hand and, bending it downward, started again. This time the serrated blade sank into the flaky black bark, soon exposing the white of the wood below.

But as Russ tried to pull the blade back, it snagged again. Grimacing, he leaned out further to add more weight to the branch. Abruptly, it snapped. He lunged at the main bough, feeling his body toppling forward into space. But his fingers couldn't extricate themselves from the saw's handle. As he started to fall a knee dislodged the hammer and he had time to think, which of us will reach the ground first? Then the forest floor was speeding towards his face. He managed to dip his head and twist so, when he hit the ground, it was with his shoulder, back and arm that had been holding the saw. He felt his legs cartwheel over and slam against the forest floor. All the air in his chest shot from his lips. There was a moment of complete silence. I'm only winded, he said to himself, knowing that the mounting sense of suffocation was going to get worse. You'll breathe again eventually, but you'll just have to wait. His mouth opened and shut as he willed his lungs to re-inflate. Come on. Come on.

'Russ?' Jim's face appeared above him. 'Russ?'

He pointed at his mouth, unable to speak.

'Winded?'

He managed a weak nod.

'Is he dead?' Andrew's voice, high and shaky, came from further away.

Russ moved a hand to his breast and weakly slapped at it. Air. He had to have air. He'd swop his set of Caran D'ache pencils for a mouthful. His Razor scooter. His Lego Millennium Falcon. Anything. He forced out a soft moan.

'Shall I sit you up?' Jim asked.

Russ was afraid he was about to cry when his sternum finally flexed. Air flooded his throat and he gratefully gulped it back.

Jim stepped round him, hooked a hand under each armpit and lifted him to a sitting position. At that point Russ noticed the underside of his left calf seemed to have merged with the blade of the saw. It looked odd, like some sort of optical illusion. Chest now heaving, he raised his knee. The tool lifted with it, but only a couple of inches. It then dropped back to the ground and fell on its side. Heavy droplets of blood immediately began pattering down on the shiny blade.

Up in the tree, Andrew let out a long scream.

CHAPTER 22

Jim and Russ looked briefly at each other. The droplets kept falling. Tap. Tap. Tap tap. Tap tap tap. A scarlet circle was pushing out across the wide, flat blade. Russ could see the saw's serrated edge was clogged at one point with small pinkish blobs.

Above them, Andrew's scream was losing power.

'Can you feel it?' Jim whispered.

'No.'

'I think it's bad.'

'Yes.'

'Should we look?'

'I don't want to.'

'We should look.'

'I don't want to.'

A bulging point in the pool's perimeter touched the edge of the blade. The mini-waterfall lasted a second before dissipating into a series of drops, similar in their frequency to the ones detaching themselves from the underside of Russ' leg. He wondered how long the process could continue before his body ran out of blood.

'We should look,' Jim repeated.

With a grim nod, Russ reached forward and began to hitch up the left leg of his tracksuit bottoms. The front of his shin was white, the tight skin slightly shiny. He twisted his leg round, allowing them a better view of the underside of his calf.

The skin covering the curved muscle wasn't smooth,

like it should be. It had a gaping mouth that grinned redly up at them. Blood was welling up out of it. What wasn't flowing silently down his leg and into his sock was dripping down onto the blade.

Above them, they heard Andrew let out a retch.

Russ looked closer. The flesh inside the wound was different; white and meaty. Like a pork chop, Russ thought. A pork chop that was able to pump out blood.

Jim also made a gagging sound as he turned away.

Russ' eyes moved to the massed patches of sunlight that suddenly trembled on the forest floor all around him. One was even dancing on the tip of his trainer. The sun must have come out, but he felt dizzy and cold. A shiver passed through him.

'The best laid plans of mice and men.'

He turned to where the voice had come from. Oh good grief, no. It was the weird woman. The one with the freakishly long hair. The one who people at school pretended to be when they played 'it'.

She was standing by the tree, an arm above her head, fingers gripping a lower branch. One knee was higher than the other. Russ saw her foot was resting on the beginnings of a root that jutted out from the trunk's base. She stepped fully down and walked calmly towards him.

For a brief, terrifying second, he wondered if Jim and Andrew might run for it, leaving him alone in the woods. With her. To his relief, they both stayed still, too surprised to do anything else.

He really didn't like her hair. It was so white and so long. Frighteningly long. Mad person long. But when she spoke, she sounded normal. There was none of the scratchy howling that people made when pretending to be her at school.

'Nasty fall, that was. I heard the thud. What's your name?'

'Russ.'

'Russ.' She was now kneeling, no thought for her long

skirt getting dirty. It was a plain green, with darker purplish patterns. She wore plimsol-like shoes with black rubbery soles. Above her dark grey socks, he saw her legs were hairy. Hairier than his.

'It's deep. Opened up a few blood vessels. A messy one, that.' She looked at his face for the first time. Her green eyes were caught in a mesh of fine wrinkles. Her lips were thin and not much different in colour to the rest of her face. He thought that, if she was his teacher, he'd never ever dare misbehave.

'What we need to do is close the wound up. That'll stop all this blood.' She leaned back and he noticed she had a kind of pouch round her waist. Like the men who ran the fruit and vegetable stall at the market wore. But hers was larger and made of a sack-like material. She glanced at Jim.

'The hammer. It's just there.'

Jim blinked. Russ glanced in the direction of her pointing finger. The tool had landed a few feet from his head.

'Come on!' she urged. 'Stir yourself.' Her chin lifted. 'And you in the tree? Down you come.'

As Jim turned to get the hammer, she extracted several wedges of different leaves from her waist pouch. Selecting one, she immediately slipped the others back out of sight. Like they were secrets.

Dark red string bound the bunch in her hand. A she undid the knot and started ripping several of them into pieces, Russ studied her hands. The skin looked horribly tough and leathery. As her fingers pinched and tore, he could see the tendons flexing in her lumpy knuckles. Meandering across the backs of her hands were fat, bluish veins.

'Lie on your side,' she said. 'So the wound is facing me and keep that leg stretched out.'

He did as he was told. Jim stepped closer, mutely holding the hammer out.

'Thank you.' Next, she placed the pieces of leaf on the blood-covered blade and, using the ball of the hammer, started mashing leaves and blood together. Russ had to twist his head in order to watch over his shoulder.

The way she rotated the hammer as she pressed down reminded him of the cookery programmes his mum liked: the chefs did the same with long oval stones and crude bowls.

Putting the hammer aside, she lifted some of the mush up with her fingers. 'Does the wound sting or does it feel numb?'

'Numb. Kind of throbs.'

'That's good. Normally, this would sting. These leaves are high in antiseptic. They also have strong anti-inflammatory properties. Probably, you'll feel a tingle.'

She applied the mixture to the wound, smearing the edges across the surrounding skin. A cool feeling crept into his lower leg.

'See the moss growing on that log?' she asked Jim. 'Peel some off and bring it to me, please.'

Jim hurried over to the horizontal length of wood and returned with a patch of spongy green in his palm.

She laid it face-down on the gooey layer. Then she lifted more leaves and placed them across the layer of moss. 'Do any of you have a mobile phone?'

No one spoke.

'I thought not. You?' She glanced up at Jim. 'Can you find your way back to the road?'

'Yeah.' He pointed off to the left. 'Down that way.'

'Correct. Go back there and – if a car passes – stop it and tell them an ambulance is needed.' She thought for a moment. 'It should go to Maggy Wallace's place. Is that clear?'

Jim sent an uneasy look at Russ, who gave him a nod. 'OK. I'll be back soon.'

Andrew sidled closer to his brother.

'Not you,' Maggy said. 'I need you to hold the poultice

in place. Come here.'

Andrew looked close to tears as he approached.

'Have you a cat or a rabbit? Something like that?' Maggy asked.

'No.'

'No pets?'

He shook his head.

'Have you ever stroked a cat or a dog?'

'Yes,' he whispered.

'When you stroked it, you pressed your hand down a bit, didn't you?'

Andrew nodded.

'I want you to press a bit harder than that. Do you understand? Not too hard, but not too lightly either.'

Andrew's looked fearfully about. His hands hung at his sides, about level with Maggy's eyes. She saw they were shaking. 'Does the sight of blood scare you?'

'Not really.'

'Are you afraid you'll be in trouble about this?'

He shook his head.

'But you're afraid about something.' She stayed still for a moment then tilted her head. 'Are you afraid of me?'

He kept his eyes averted.

She smiled. 'Well, there's nothing unusual about that. But I'll tell you a secret, if you promise to keep it. I'm not really scary – even though I look it. Stops people bothering me, see?'

He risked a quick glance at her.

She raised a finger to her lips. 'Keep that between us. Now, when I move my hand, you take its place.'

Crouching, Andrew reached a hand out.

'After three,' she said. 'One, two, three.'

They swopped and she stood. 'Well done.' She glanced at Jim and the hardness was back in her voice. 'Why are you still here? Go!'

He wrenched his eyes from the strange scene then jogged off between the trees. Russ felt himself shiver as he continued to watch the woman.

She reached into her pouch once again and produced a small knife with a black handle. Lifting the hem of her long dress, she cut through it and then tore the lowermost couple of inches away. Once she'd wrapped the ribbon of material around the layer of leaves, she looked off into the trees. 'I'm worried about shock.'

A second or two went by before Russ realised she'd been speaking to him. 'I'm fine, honest.'

'No. You're beginning to shiver.' She looked down at him. 'And you're very pale.' She turned to Andrew. 'Is his face normally that white?'

Andrew still looked terrified of speaking. 'No.'

'Can almost see his bones,' she murmured. 'I was going to nip back to mine and wait for the paramedics. But that's not going to work. They could be ages and you need warmth. We'll have to walk you there instead.' She glanced at Andrew. 'Can you collect all the tools together? I'm going to find your friend a crutch.'

'I can hop,' Russ said, beginning to sit up.

'Stay where you are,' she shot back, walking purposefully through the trees. 'Hopping is a silly idea. It'll raise your heart rate and set off fresh bleeding. I shan't be long.'

Once she was out of earshot, Andrew squatted down. 'Can you run for it?'

He looked at the younger boy. 'Run for it? Why?'

'To get away from her.'

'Get away? She's helping me. I'm not running anywhere.'

Andrew didn't look happy.

'Where did she come from, anyway?' Russ asked. 'I didn't hear her coming.'

'That's because she wasn't on the ground.'

'What do you mean?'

He pointed into the tree. 'She was up there. Above us.'

Russ lifted his eyebrows. 'No.'

'She was!' Andrew checked to make sure she wasn't coming back. 'That's why we need to get away. She's not...natural.'

'You're off your head. No way could she – '

'You fell. Then there was all that blood. Next thing, she was climbing down past me. Really fast.'

Russ remembered the younger boy's shrieks abruptly halting. He looked up into the tree. Jagged sunlight spangled his eyes. He squinted. The cedar tree was tall – but the pine trees around it were taller. The cedar's upper branches interlinked with those of its neighbours. They merged with the next ones along to form a thick ceiling.

He recalled seeing her for the first time. One hand had been gripping the branch above her, like she'd just clambered to the ground. Has she made her way through the canopy to spy on them from up high? Or had she been perched up there all along?

He dismissed the thought. Andrew had been panicking. He'd got it wrong. The woman was fifty, maybe sixty. Miles older than his mum. Old women didn't climb trees.

'She's coming back,' Andrew hissed.

Moments later, she was beside them. In her hand was a stout branch, the top splitting neatly off in two like a pair of stubby horns. 'That looks good,' she murmured. 'I'll help you to your feet. Keep one arm around my shoulders and one arm over the crutch. The idea is you don't need to put any weight on your bad leg.'

He felt himself lifted, surprised by her strength. She ducked under his arm and draped it over her shoulder. It was bony and hard. As her left hand passed him the crutch, her right arm encircled his waist. He could feel her slender bicep pressing into his ribs and suddenly he had no problem imagining her up in those trees, moving from branch to branch like some white-haired, wizen-faced marmoset.

CHAPTER 23

'I want to, Mum.'

'Russ, why would you want to go back up there? You said your thanks when the ambulance arrived, didn't you?'

'Not properly, not really.'

His mum sighed. 'She's not a normal person, Russ. You do realise that? Folk say she likes to kill animals out in those woods.'

'I know. But I think that's rubbish. She had this tame bird. It sat on her shoulder like a parrot. Really cool it was.'

His mum's attention drifted back to the TV screen. The camera was on some young people. They were gathered in a lodge that overlooked an empty beach. Even though the girls wore bikinis and the blokes swimming shorts, they all had canvas belts with little black boxes. Wires trailed up naked torsos and looped round necks.

She loves these reality type programmes, he thought. The setting for this one looked amazing, he had to admit. But all they did was form little groups, wave their arms about and sound angry. Why did they spend all their time arguing? They could have been snorkelling or building sandcastles or collecting shells.

'Mum? The ambulance men said I should be grateful.'

She spoke while still watching the screen. 'Yeah, and they also had no idea what that shit was she slapped all over your leg.'

'They said it could have been very serious if she – '

'I know, I know.' She sent him a withering look. 'I'm not trekking up there. And you're not meant to be walking about.'

From the corner of the room came an ugly noise: grating hacks, repeated one after the other. Russ winced.

His Mum was instantly on her feet. 'Otto, in the kitchen! Out! Out!' Bending forward, hands clapping together at knee height, she paced quickly towards the chair in the corner. A tortoiseshell cat staggered out from behind it, back hunched and mouth wide open in a grimace.

'Not in here!' she almost shouted. 'Out!'

The animal moved reluctantly towards the door, torso convulsing as if the floor carried an electric charge. A particularly loud cough stopped it in its tracks. Its head dropped and it deposited a slime-covered pellet on the carpet. As soon as the object fell from its mouth, the animal shot into the kitchen. The cat flap clacked shut a second later.

'Little bastard,' she sighed, turning away from the slug-shaped lump of fur. 'Russ? Could you? You know how it makes me – '

He reached for an old copy of *Bella* lying next to him on the sofa. 'There's a track. The ambulance managed to get all the way to her place.'

'A track?'

'Yes.'

'You know where the turning off the road is, to get on this track?'

'Yes.' He curved the magazine into a scoop, but didn't get up. 'Can we?'

She placed her hands on her hips. 'We're not staying long, all right?'

The car rolled to a stop. 'This,' she stated incredulously, 'is where she lives?'

Russ nodded, eyes on the smoke trailing from the

chimney. 'She must be in. It's really cosy inside. And she has all these books and other stuff on her shelves.'

'We're not going in. You say your thanks outside and we'll be on our way.'

He gave a resigned nod.

As they approached the door, a bird swooped down from a nearby tree. It alighted on the gutter's edge and angled one beady eye down at them.

'That's it,' Russ pointed excitedly. 'Like a parrot with its blue feathers. See them, on the wings where they join its body?'

His mum regarded the bird with narrowed eyes. 'Why's it staring at us?'

'Probably thinks we've got food.'

They were within touching distance of the door when it swung inward. Her face appeared from the gloom, mouth open, something sharp ready on her lips. She recognised Russ and her expression immediately softened. 'It's you.'

'Hello Mrs Wallace.'

Her gaze moved to his leg. 'How's it healing? You're standing well on it.'

'We can't stay,' his mum cut in.

The two women regarded each other. Maggy seemed to acknowledge something before turning her attention back to Russ. 'How many stitches?'

'You were nearly right. Twenty three. And eight on the inside, too. But it's all bandaged up, so I can't show you.'

She stepped out and the door swung almost shut behind her. 'Thirty-one stitches. A good number.'

'Thank you for your help.' The statement was a little wooden, but he held eye contact as he made it.

She inclined her head a fraction. 'I appreciate you coming out here to let me know.'

'Well, then...' Russ' mum said. 'We ought to be – '

A whirr of wings broke her sentence. The bird, now standing on Maggy Wallace's shoulder, let out a croak.

'See!' Russ looked delightedly up at his mum. 'Isn't it

like a parrot?'

Maggy lifted a finger and ran the back of it down the bird's breast. 'Probably the closest thing to a parrot in these parts. Remember what it is, Russ?'

He screwed his face up. 'Ja – Jackdaw? No, they're black.'

'Close. From the crow family. It's a Jay.'

'Jay! That's it. She found it, Mum. Raised it from a chick.'

'That's...interesting.' His mum managed a brittle smile.

'And over there,' he pointed to an H shaped structure of timber. Each head-high upright was topped by a flat square of wood. 'That's the Pine Martens' feeding station.'

The Jay flew through the gap in Maggy's front door. She lifted her chin. 'And the box up in that tree, Russ? Remember who lives – '

'Bats! They crawl in through the opening at the bottom.'

She smiled. 'I wasn't sure you were taking it all in. But I didn't want you to nod off.' She looked at Russ' mum. 'The ambulance was a long while arriving.'

'Yes, I heard.' Her lips twitched. 'Er, thanks for taking care of him. I can tell you, it's the last time he goes wandering off – '

'He can come back anytime.'

Russ' mum paused in the act of turning round. 'That's very – '

'I mean it. He's a bright boy. Polite. He's welcome anytime.'

'OK,' she looked back at her car. 'That's something to think about. Definitely.'

'Mum?' Russ could tell she wasn't taking the offer seriously. He couldn't quite say why, but the thought of spending time out here thrilled him. 'When you go to see Gerry on a Saturday? I could visit then. It would be better than staying in on my own.'

The comment caused his mum's face to redden. Her

eyes flicked guiltily in Maggy's direction.

'I can show him these woods,' Maggy said. 'So he can be safe.'

Russ' mum looked about uncertainly. The forest stretched off in all directions. She felt like, if she said no, it would surge across the track behind them, trapping her forever.

'Please Mum?'

'Only while it's light. You have to be home before its dark.'

Russ glanced excitedly at Maggy. 'So I can, then?'

'If that's what you want,' his mum finally said.

CHAPTER 24

Russ tried to walk, like the doctor had told him to – but the desire to get there was just too strong. He broke into a jog, and as he listened to his trainers connecting with the track that led to Maggy's cabin, his mind leapt from image to image. She had shown him so much. Things that existed under his very nose, but he'd never noticed. Or, if he had, he'd never stopped to think. To really think.

They'd started in what passed for her garden. Slowly, methodically, she'd led him along each row of plants. She seemed to be growing every type of vegetable he couldn't stand: Brussels sprouts and cabbage, curly kale and turnips. He made himself pay attention and sound interested. But this stuff: he could see it in the allotments any time he wanted.

Youthful eyes twinkling in her wrinkled face, she'd eventually announced that it was time for something more interesting.

As she'd veered suddenly towards the tree line, he'd wondered if it had been some kind of test. Like, if he'd not made an effort to listen, she'd have shown him back to the track and said goodbye. He thought it might have been.

Where the clearing grew more unkempt, she paused, finger held towards a cluster of waist-high plants. 'Do you know what these are?'

The plants had lost the columns of purple flowers that lined their long stems during the summer, but he knew what they were. 'Foxgloves.'

'Correct. Did you know they can kill you?'

He didn't.

'Digitalis – that's the lively bit of this plant. It's active principle. In small doses, it can be very useful. It's used in some heart medicines nowadays. Too much though, and you won't feel well. Not well at all.'

She'd continued towards the forest's edge, stopping where the grass thinned beneath the sprawling boughs of a massive oak tree. Reaching up, she plucked something from the end of a twig and held it out. 'This?'

He'd seen them before, too. Little balls of wood, each punctured by a perfect hole. 'Some kind of a seed?'

'What are the seeds of an oak tree called?'

He sagged inwardly, knowing his guess had not been thought through. 'Acorns.'

'But this is not an acorn.'

Of course it wasn't. So how come she'd picked it off the end of a branch? He looked up and could see others clinging to the twigs like little baubles. He'd never really considered what they could be.

She handed it to him. 'It's known as an oak apple. As you can see, it's no type of fruit.'

He looked at her expectantly.

'There's a type of small wasp. Oak apples are created by its larvae.'

'You mean grubs?'

'Yes. In the spring, the female wasp injects an egg into the mid-rib of a newly-growing leaf. The larva hatches – a mere dot of a thing – and releases a chemical. The chemical is rather clever; it reacts with the inside of the mid-rib and prompts the tree to form a hard casing – or what's known as a gall – around the larva. So, what's in your hand is actually a mutated leaf. At first, the gall is just a little bobble. As the larva feeds on the leaf tissue growing inside, it gets bigger – and so does the gall. When the larva is fully-grown, it turns into a pupa – and then an adult wasp. The wasp bores its way out of the gall using its mandibles, flies away, and the process begins again next spring.'

Russ held the oak apple close to his face and regarded the hole. It was perfectly round. He wanted to slice it in half to see within. 'Can I keep it? Take it into science?'

'If you like. Another type of wasp – also very small – makes zombies out of ladybirds.'

Russ looked up. 'Zombies? Like the monsters?'

'Creatures that have had their free-will stolen. Those zombies.'

'A wasp does that?' This was feeling like a lesson, but a good one. 'How?'

Her hand dipped through the air. 'This type of wasp swoops down on an unsuspecting ladybird and – quick as a flash – jabs it with its stinger. Along with several chemicals, something else is injected into the ladybird. What do you think that might be?'

'A larva?'

'An egg, actually. The chemicals create a little cavity, the egg hatches and the larva lives off fluids that seep into its home. The ladybird doesn't know it, but it has a parasite – and everything it eats only helps its parasite to grow. Has the ladybird actually been taken over by the wasp larva by this stage? We don't know. But, by the next stage, it definitely has.'

The sounds of the forest were fading; all he heard were her words.

'When the larva is ready to develop into an adult, it squeezes back out through a gap in the ladybird's exoskeleton. Does the ladybird turn on this fat, juicy, helpless morsel and devour it? No. Because now, the ladybird is a slave. It remains perfectly still while the larva spins a dense cocoon between its legs. The ladybird then guards this cocoon – if a predator comes too close, it waves its legs about to warn it off. After a week, the adult wasp cuts its way out of the cocoon and,' she fluttered her fingers, 'away it flies.'

'And the ladybird?'

'Most stay standing there until they die. The odd one seems to recover its senses and wanders off.'

Russ examined the oak apple in his palm. He looked back at Maggy with narrowed eyes. 'The larva that lived in here, it did something similar. Fooled the tree into growing it a shell, somewhere safe to develop?'

She snapped her fingers. 'He's quick! He's agile!' She jumped from one foot to the other. 'He has mental agility, this boy!'

The sight of woman her age hopping about like that; he couldn't help giggle.

'What do ladybirds like to eat?' she asked, standing still once more.

He knew this: he'd watched one once, making its way along the stem of a plant, snaffling the little green creatures in its path. 'Aphids!'

'Good. And what do aphids eat?'

'I'm not sure.'

She brandished her arms above her head.

His eyes swept the bare branches. 'Trees?'

'Leaves, more accurately. The suck the sap out of leaves – including those belonging to oak trees.' She glanced up at the branches. 'Oak trees talk, you know. They warn each other when aphids are on the attack.'

He shot a dubious look at the bulging trunk, the cracked armour of bark.

'The oak tree releases tannin – a very bitter substance – into its leaves. This makes them taste horrible to aphids. But the oak tree doesn't stop there; it also releases a special kind of scent into the air. A pheromone. Oak trees nearby,' she pointed to another further round the clearing, 'pick up this warning and also flood their leaves with tannin. Amazing, don't you think?' She began to circle slowly round. 'Wasps hatch out of ladybirds. Ladybirds eat aphids. Aphids eat oak leaves. Oak leaves attract ladybirds. Ladybirds attract wasps. Everything is connected, you see.

Everything is linked by invisible strands. And these strands,' she pushed a long trail of hair back over her shoulder, 'these strands are all around us. You just have to look.' She faced him once again. 'Now, let's go inside – I could do with a cup of tea.'

Russ didn't move. His eyes were on the oak apple, lips pursed in thought.

'Question?'

'You said chemicals released by the wasp larva got the tree to create this?'

'Correct.'

'But the tree didn't know?'

'Perhaps it did. Trees are very benign. They wouldn't begrudge a few leaves for wasp larvae. After all, wasps are partial to aphids.'

'What I mean is, the tree doesn't have a brain. It didn't say to itself, "I know, I'll mutate this leaf into a little hard ball."'

'I suppose not.'

'But...with the zombie ladybird, how does that work?'

She leaned down so their eyes were level. 'Go on.'

His lips moved against each other, like he was sucking a sweet. 'How...how does the larva control the ladybird's actual behaviour? Make it decide to just stand there?'

A mysterious smile was lighting her face. 'What do you think?'

'I don't know. With chemicals, I suppose.'

She gave a clap. 'You, my friend, have just jumped clean beyond school. You have landed in evolutionary biology. Right now, people are at university doing doctorates on this stuff. You're correct: chemicals. What the wasp injects into the ladybird contains a powerful cocktail of chemicals. Some of these chemicals work their way into the ladybird's brain. Once there, they target certain genes. You've heard of genes?'

'Kind of, we get them from our mum and dad. They decide how we look.'

'Some do, yes. The wasp's chemicals home in on the genes that control the ladybird's behaviour. By making these genes mutate, the wasp wins control of the ladybird. Now,' she rubbed her hands together, 'it really is time for some tea.'

They'd walked a few steps before he stopped again. 'What are genes made of?'

Her laugh was loud and full of delight. 'Next time you visit? We can discuss genes.'

Russ slowed to a walk. How far had he just jogged? He scanned the track ahead. There was her cabin, showing between the trees. For the past week, all he'd thought about was their conversation. Genes. He'd tried to look up information on the internet. He'd read that genes drove behaviour. Did that mean they contained the knowledge a beaver needed to gnaw down trees and build a dam? That allowed a tiny spider to construct such impossibly intricate webs? That swung a turtle slowly round to cross vast oceans back to the exact beach where it was born? Did genes do all that?

So much of what he'd read was beyond him; he needed Maggy to explain it.

As he reached the clearing, he spotted the jay up on the cabin roof. The clearing seemed oddly quiet. Not even the wooden chimes stirred. The jay studied him as he walked down the path. 'Hi,' he called to it. 'Where's Maggy?'

The bird cocked its head.

'In here?' He gestured at the closed door. 'Is she?' He reached the front step. 'Maggy, it's me, Russ. Are you there?'

No reply.

As he knocked on the door, he caught a whiff of something. His nose automatically wrinkled: like when Mum forgot about bacon in the fridge. 'Maggy?'

He turned the handle, pushed the door open and the smell hit him properly.

CHAPTER 25

Father Ian Thompson looked around restlessly. His throat felt dry and itchy. There was a small kitchen near the front entrance, next to the room the Sunday school used. But it meant walking the entire length of the dark church; fumbling about for light switches; hunting about for milk that was still fresh; filling the kettle and boiling it.

It also meant prolonging the other man's presence. Enduring the sharp tang of his body odour for even longer. The desire to be free of it – and Crowther himself – was more acute than any thirst. He turned back to his visitor, knowing he wouldn't leave until he'd recounted the rest of his story. 'So, who – or what – was next on Sullivan's list?'

Crowther looked . 'How do you mean?'

'I presume your photographer friend hasn't stopped there?'

Crowther drew a hand across his mouth and jaw, as if assessing the need to shave. 'No.'

'Yet, he's sold you the pictures of Mandy's death. The story has run in your magazine. He's got his money. Why all this subsequent activity? What exactly does he want to achieve?'

Crowther looked bemused, as if the priest's question was patently obvious. 'He's intrigued by events. I mean, the fact that what connects the deaths of Gregory Lang and Mandy Cost is Maggy Wallace's hair – '

'Come on. You and him – this is going to be another story, isn't it?' Thompson leaned back, arms still crossed. The glare of the light seemed to be bothering Crowther; he squirmed in his seat. This visit, Thompson thought, is part of the project.

'It's not a financial thing, what he's doing,' Crowther finally announced.

'Really?' Thompson shot back. 'Did he take his camera with him?'

'Yes.'

Just as Thompson suspected. 'So he's taking photographs of people and places that featured in Mandy Cost's life.'

Crowther's chin came up. 'Mandy Cost? This isn't about Mandy Cost.'

'Oh no?' Thompson arched an eyebrow.

The remark seemed to aggravate Crowther. 'Why are you going on about Mandy bloody Cost?' he demanded, sending a resentful look up at the light shining down on him.

'Isn't that where the photographer is now? Sniffing around Mandy's home town, maybe? Seeking out childhood friends for gossip?'

Crowther shook his head. 'It's not about her! Joe's gone to where Maggy Wallace used to teach. The town she lived in for over twenty years.'

Thompson blinked. It wasn't the response he'd been expecting. 'Why would he do that?'

'Because the story's shifted – it's now about Maggy Wallace. Christ, can't you see that?'

'You've no interest in Mandy Cost's story? That's what you're claiming?'

Crowther placed his hands on the table. 'OK, initially, Joe Sullivan had proposed a follow-up on Mandy. A kind of biography in pictures – we had discussed that, yes.'

I knew it, Thompson thought. The truth at last. He could imagine the childhood snaps of Mandy. People would love to follow how that innocent person ended up as a crop-haired corpse on a London pavement. And his church would feature in the account. The fact she'd come and seen him so often. Crowther said something. 'Sorry?' Thompson asked.

'With Sullivan, his mind works in images. They're what he does. His way of communicating.'

'And these images he's been taking – you expect me to believe they're only for him? A visual record, some sort of a photo album: that's what you're saying?'

'We're all visual animals, aren't we? At heart,' Crowther murmured, eyes touching Thompson's for a brief moment.

What, Thompson thought, did he mean by that? He ran his tongue across his teeth, uneasiness robbing his mouth of saliva. Did Crowther know everything? Had Mandy spoken to the photographer about her visits? The informal confessions he'd invited her to make, the things he'd asked her to describe? Guilt swept through Thompson's mind. He struggled to keep control of his face. Don't be stupid, he told himself. Even if Mandy had confided in the photographer, how could it connect to the other thing? The thing that must stay hidden. She didn't know about that. And if she didn't, how could Crowther and Sullivan?

At that moment, he could see the locked door of the upstairs room in his house. The door only he could open. What was inside – his secret – was safe. Known only to him. 'You've lost me here. What are you saying?'

'I was pointing out the power pictures have.' Crowther gestured at the wall-hanging across the room. 'That thing. Someone's spent hours weaving that image. Loaves of bread, some fish. A picture has immediacy. Power. Same as the stained glass windows in your church, I suppose.'

Thompson contemplated the table as he turned the other man's words over in his mind, searching them for hidden meanings. He couldn't decide if they contained anything, or not. Suddenly, he'd had enough. The two men were planning a feature on Mandy Cost's life, however much Crowther claimed otherwise. A feature that would include his church. For all he knew, Sullivan was waiting outside with his damn camera. It was time, the priest decided, for Crowther to leave. 'Right, it's late. I need to lock up. You can use this door. The path will take –'

'But I haven't told you everything. There's more.'

'I don't think there is. In fact, I think I've given you too long as it is.' He started sweeping the photos into a pile.

Crowther turned his head towards the door. 'But – '

'No, sorry. I'm not prepared to sit here any longer.'

'Something's happened to Joe.'

Thompson paused in the act of stacking of images on top of the folder. This was Crowther trying anything, now. Anything to stretch things out.

'Every time I ring,' Crowther said urgently, 'I get his answer phone. He should have called me back by now.'

Both Thompson's hands were on the table, palms pressing down in readiness to stand.

'For pity's sake, hear me out!' Crowther pleaded.

The look of utter despair was back in his eyes. Emotion like that, Thompson thought, was extremely hard to fake. 'How long has it been since you've been ringing?'

'About three hours? Last time I rang him was just before coming in here.'

'Three hours?' Thompson said. 'That's hardly cause for concern.'

'I've left him eight messages, easily.'

'Which might mean his phone's out of battery.'

'He carries spares. So he's always contactable. I'm telling you, something's wrong.'

Suppressing a sigh, Thompson sank back on his chair. 'Might he be at home, asleep or something?'

'No. He was travelling to the town where Maggy Wallace lived, remember?'

Thompson nodded. 'Perhaps his phone's been lost or mislaid en route.'

'He called me earlier this afternoon. When he first got there. Left a message. This place near Middlesborough. Here.' He took his phone from his pocket and laid it on the table. An unsteady finger pressed a couple of buttons.

Thompson bowed his head to avoid the other man's anxious stare. A mechanical sounding female voice announced the message had been received today at 2:04 pm. There was a pause, then a throaty male voice with a heavy London accent began to speak.

'Nigel, it's Joe here. I'm, um...' He gave a bewildered half-laugh. 'I'm outside the school where Maggy Wallace used to teach. It's half-term. The place is deserted, but...er...I'm looking across at this oak tree out in the middle of the playing fields. You won't believe this, but someone's in the lower branches. They're in shadow, so I can't really make them out...hang on, movement. The person's climbing down...climbing down bloody fast, too. Christ mate, I think...think it's her.'

Thompson looked up. Nigel Crowther was trembling. A strand of black hair had slipped forward and was plastered across his glistening forehead.

'It is...I really think it is. I can see her, Nigel. Maggy Wallace: she's standing on the bloody grass! Oh Jesus, I can...' Panic lifted his voice. 'She's coming, she's coming.' Something – maybe Joe's fingers – made contact with the mouthpiece. The sound was like a muffled roll of thunder. 'The keys! Where are my fucking keys! Oh my God, oh no, oh no, no – '

CHAPTER 26

Silence.

Thompson stared at the phone. He had to remind himself this was all a ruse. A monstrous trick, designed to unsettle him, force him into making some kind of admission about Mandy. Yes. That's what it was. He looked across the table.

Crowther was hunched forward, elbows tucked in, his bunched fingers seeking refuge beneath his chin. A hand reached for the phone, then stopped as if the casing might burn him. The woman's voice sounded. Press five to hear the message again. 'Do you want to?' he whispered.

'No.'

A finger quickly pressed the red button, severing the call.

'That's it? Thompson asked. 'That's your last contact?'

Crowther nodded. 'Now I just get his answer phone.'

'I don't know what you want from me. Really, I don't.' Thompson's voice was flat. 'All this you've told me, do you want my opinion? Is that it? Do you want to know what I think?'

When Crowther spoke, his voice was barely audible. 'I want you to help me.'

'Help you? How would you like me to help you?'

'I've been so stupid. I don't know why I did such a – '

'Tell me: how am I supposed to help you?'

'I'm in danger.'

'If you genuinely believe that, why not go to the police?'

Crowther's eyes were wide. Microscopic veins formed a pinkish halo round his irises. 'Gregory Lang went to the police! He still wasn't safe. She got to him, even when he was locked up.'

The priest spoke with a calm authority. For him, this was an area of familiarity: dealing with irrational fears. Demons of the mind. 'You believe Maggy Wallace was responsible for Gregory Lang's suicide?'

'And Mandy Cost's! And whatever's happened to Joe. Can't you see what's happening?'

'I understand what you think is happening.'

'No!' Crowther raked back his hair with both hands. 'Please don't give me that psycho-analysis approach.'

'I didn't mean to.'

'You're not concerned?' Crowther waved a hand back and forth. 'You're happy to just sit there? After all I've told you?'

Thompson waited for the other man to settle. 'I am concerned. I can see this is causing you distress. What if we try to establish the whereabouts of Joe? I think with that, you'll be reassured. At the moment, you're assuming something's happened to Joe, you're seeing an escalation of events, and so – '

'You agree she was a witch?'

'Maggy Wallace?'

Crowther bobbed his head up and down. 'She was a witch. When Gregory Lang killed her, she was gripping that little dagger. Maybe she wasn't evil during her life. But, as she died, she was mumbling stuff: he saw her lips moving. What if it was a curse or a spell or something?' Tears were making their way down his cheeks. Fresh waves of sour sweat filled the air. 'Something dark, something powerful enough so she could come back. And now, now she has! And everyone will pay, including me.' He wiped at his face with jerky fingers. 'I am going to die.'

Thompson raised both hands. 'You are not going to die. Joe Sullivan will call you – or we'll establish his whereabouts – and you'll see these concerns are based purely on fear. Nothing more.'

Crowther's teeth emerged in a semblance of a smile. 'This calmness, is it because of your beliefs? You know you're safe because God will protect you?'

Thompson placed his hands in his lap. 'That question contains a number of assumptions. To believe I'm safe means I accept there's a threat to my safety. That means acknowledging the ghost of Maggy Wallace, along with a vengeful nature.'

'But you said earlier, when we were sat out there,' his glance touched the door leading back into the church, 'you said you believe people have a soul. When I asked you, you said you did.'

'There's a world of difference between that and what you're claiming. Now, as I said, we need to shine some rational light onto all of this. And the best way to do that is by establishing contact with Joe Sullivan.'

Crowther shifted in his seat. 'Can I use the toilet?'

'Of course.'

Crowther got out of his seat. Thompson watched as he slowly crossed the room on stiff legs. If this was an act, he thought, it was amazingly good. The toilet door shut. Thompson stared at it. Mandy Cost had died in very odd circumstances; she'd also just been administered a pain-killing injection. Gregory Lang had also died an unusual death. But the person was facing a murder charge and had been taking large quantities of drugs. His mind obviously unbalanced.

Thompson's eyes shifted to the folder of photos. The one of the broken window was top of the pile. The ghostly face was undoubtedly disturbing – but it was just like hundreds of other images that existed on the internet. They were fake, as the people responsible for them often admitted. In skilled hands, computers made wonderful tools.

The toilet flushed and he looked at the door. Whose hands had manipulated the image on the table?

Crowther had left his attaché case on the third chair. Thompson had noticed the other man occasionally glancing at it. The top of it was partly open. Was something hidden inside? Was Crowther recording their conversation? Was that why the top of it was open?

He checked the toilet door again. Firmly shut. He heard a tap turning on.

Thompson rose from his seat. The gap at the top of the attaché was too narrow and dark for him to see in. He'd have to open it wider. Placing one hand half-way across the table, he leaned forward and reached for the case. His outstretched fingers were inches away when the screen of Crowther's phone came to life. A nanosecond later, it began to ring. Thompson's hand shot back. The glass panel was glowing pale blue, a name clearly visible in the middle.

Joe Sullivan.

CHAPTER 27

'Who is it?' Crowther was coming out of the toilet, wiping wet hands on his trousers.

'It says Joe Sullivan.'

The other man's mouth opened in surprise. He bounded across the room and snatched the phone up. 'Joe?'

All Thompson could hear was a intermittent digital hum as someone spoke.

Crowther started to frown. 'You what?'

More words. Thompson turned an ear. Nothing was distinct, but the comment ended with an upward inflection. A question.

'I'm a friend of Joe's, yes,' Crowther replied uncertainly.

Something else was said. Crowther was staring in Thompson's direction, but his eyes didn't seem focused. 'Yes. I have been calling him, yes. What's going on?' He listened again. 'Is...is he OK? No, I don't. He didn't have much contact with them. No wife. A sister, he has a sister. Sade. How did it happen? Please, tell me...OK. The James Cook University Hospital? OK?'

As his hand slowly lowered, the phone's screen went out. Crowther remained standing, as if in a trance.

'Who was that speaking?' Thompson asked.

Crowther suddenly appeared to see him. 'A policeman. From Darlington.' He pulled his chair back and slumped into it.

With a last furtive glance down at the attaché case, Thompson also sat down. 'What did he say?'

'Joe's crashed his motorbike into a tree. By that school. I was the last person he'd dialled. They wanted the number of someone in his family.'

Thompson sat forward. 'Did they say how he was?'

'No, he wouldn't tell me. But Joe wasn't wearing his helmet.' He regarded his phone for a second and put it on the table. 'You heard the message he left me. She was coming for him, he must have got his bike started, then he's lost...oh shit...'

Thompson crossed his legs. Something light and airy was shifting in his lower stomach. Fear. He pressed his hands into his gut to stop it moving about. 'The officer told you which hospital he was going to. The James Cook University Hospital, correct?'

Crowther blinked. 'The James Cook University Hospital. Did he?'

'That's what you said. The officer obviously gave you it.' Thompson wasn't sure if Crowther was about to throw up or pass out.

'Did he? Yes, he probably did. He must have.' He paused. 'She got him.' His voice was a whisper. 'She got him and now she'll be coming for me.'

Thompson injected some aggression into his voice, as much for his own benefit as for Crowther's. 'We're going to call that hospital. We're going to find out how your friend is.'

'It's no use. It's no use.' He bent forward, one hand rubbing furiously at the back of his neck

'Yes it is. Do you hear me? Nigel!'

The sound of his name being barked caused Crowther to lift his head. 'You have to help me. Give me your blessing. Pray for me.' He looked wildly about. 'Have you got Holy Water in here? You could confirm me! Could you confirm me?'

'I am not about to confirm you, Nigel.'

The other man wasn't listening. 'You must have Holy Water.' He looked over at the desk. 'You could put some on me with a blessing. Yes! Splash it over my head. Is it in – '

'Nigel, I want you to pick up your phone and call that hospital. Find out when your friend was admitted and how he is.'

'He's already dead! She's killing everyone. She's going to kill me unless you – '

'You won't ring that hospital?'

Crowther clasped his head in both hands. 'Oh Jesus Christ.'

Thompson looked at the other man. He was coming apart. If this went on, he'd become hysterical. Thompson stood. 'I'm going to make us both a drink. Some tea. Nigel? I won't be long. The kitchen is close to where you came into the church, by the main doors.'

Crowther was rocking back and forth.

'Five minutes, OK? I'll be back in five.' As he stepped towards the door, Thompson pictured the long walk down the dark aisle. Christ on his crucifix would be an vague smear in the gloom, at best. The circular door handle squeaked as he turned it.

'No! Keep it closed!'

Thompson looked back. Crowther was still in his seat, head lifted just clear of his cupped hands. All his bottom teeth showed as he spoke. 'Don't leave me, please don't leave me.'

The priest half-turned. 'I'm only going to the other end of the church. I think both of us are dehydrated, not thinking properly. You can stay here, it's fine.' He continued to twist the old ring.

'Do not open that door! You mustn't, you mustn't!'

Once again, the sheer intensity of the man's emotion made Thompson hesitate. He took his fingers off the metal. 'OK, Nigel, it's OK.' He held his hand up. 'I'm not touching it.'

Crowther was breathing in and out rapidly through his nose.

Thompson retreated from the door. If I can't leave the room, he thought, it'll have to be Plan B. 'Let me call the hospital and get this cleared up.'

Crowther tracked him with desperate eyes. 'I don't think I've got long.'

Thompson picked up the ancient model's heavy plastic receiver and pressed the buttons for directory enquiries.

'There isn't time for this,' Crowther moaned. 'There isn't time.'

Thompson raised the receiver to his ear, wondering whether he should actually be calling the fast response team at the local mental health unit. It looked like it was going that way. The call was connected and a recorded voice said an operator should be with him in under two minutes.

Crowther lowered his forehead to the table and began to sob, fingers now interlinked tightly across the back of his neck.

Thompson kept the phone pressed to his ear. Ridiculous music tinkled down the line. 'Nigel? Take some deep breaths. Try to picture somewhere peaceful. Wide, open space. Clear sky. The sense of peace and quiet – '

Crowther lifted his head a few inches then slammed it against the table top.

Oh my God, Thompson thought. He's copying what Greg Lang did in the cell up in Glasgow. The voice said an operator would be available in one minute. Crowther hit his head against the table again, even harder.

'Nigel? Nigel? Listen to me, Nigel.'

His head rose again, as if his fingers were lifting it up. Thompson was just able to see the other man's eyes were tightly shut before his head pistoned down. The sound of the impact filled the small room.

I'm going to have to hang-up, Thompson thought. The

man needs help. He replaced the receiver, moved back to the table and placed a hand on Crowther's head. The sharp smell rising off him lanced the priest's nostrils. The man's hair felt greasy and damp. 'Nigel – '

'He's dead. I know he's dead!' Crowther's voice was starting to fracture and tear. 'That day when Mandy went through that window, they all started rushing about and some of the staff came outside, people were crying. Customers. It was a total mess.'

He gulped in air, trying to regain control of his voice.

'That's good,' Thompson said. 'Take deep breaths.' He smoothed his hand over the sticky black strands on Crowther's head.

'Joe, he...he went into the salon, trying to ask questions. No one was in control. It was inside that he found the hair extensions.'

Thompson reached for his chair up and placed it closer to Crowther. 'I'm listening,' he said, getting ready to sit.

'Maggy Wallace's hair – it was there, laid out neatly in a long plastic wrapper.' Crowther started sobbing again. 'He took it.'

Thompson paused, knees flexed. His legs straightened. The fluttery thing was stirring in his stomach again, more strongly this time. 'He took it? Why?'

Crowther looked up at him, eyes red with tears. 'He doesn't know. He said it just...happened.'

Thompson didn't know why his heart had suddenly started to hammer. 'And Sullivan still has the hair?'

Crowther turned his head one way then the other. 'When he set off for Scotland, he left it with me.'

It's in your possession, Thompson thought. No wonder you're petrified. 'Is it in your home, Maggy's hair?'

'No.'

'Then, where?'

A finger was waved in the direction of the third chair. Thompson looked down at the attaché case in horror. He hadn't been on a fairground ride for five decades, yet what he felt now brought those distant memories surging back. 'You vile, despicable, bastard.' He tried to move away, but had to grab the edge of the table to regain his balance. The lurching sensation wouldn't leave. Like a drunken man, he lifted the attaché case. It felt empty as he brought it down heavily on the table.

Crowther shrank back in his seat. 'I'm so sorry.'

Thompson wanted to slap his snot-riven face. Instead, he pulled the case fully open. Inside it a long sheath of cellophane lay folded in half. Similar, he thought, to the ones shops used for hanging men's ties in.

Inside it was a length of almost white hair.

Thompson started to reach in, then hesitated. To his surprise, he was reluctant to actually touch it. It was a primal fear, like the way a hand recoils at the sight of a snake, or scorpion or spider. He tried to rationalise things but his arm refused to move. He could only stare down at the package. Inside it was the thing Maggy Wallace had held most precious. She hadn't been bothered with make-up, or nice clothes or painted nails. But she did care about her hair. She was fiercely protective about her hair. Blood roared in his ears.

'What was that?' Crowther's eyes darted about.

Thompson turned on the other man. 'Take this,' he shoved the case across the table, 'and get out of my church. Get out! Now!'

Crowther was looking up at the low ceiling, mouth partly open.

Thompson grasped the man's collar and yanked him to his feet. "Get out! Get out of here!'

Crowther twisted free, staggering back a couple of steps. 'What's that noise?'

Thompson was about to reach for him again when he heard it, too. A faint rasping. A scraping whisper. He gestured at the wall-hanging. 'Pigeons, up in the tower. Now take that attaché – '

Crowther stared fearfully at the expanse of material.

His voice was little more than a croak. 'What's behind there?'

'The stairs, leading up,' Thompson replied matter-of-factly. He picked the case off the table and thrust it into the other man's arms. 'Now I asked you to – '

The noise came again, louder this time. Crowther swept his eyes across the ceiling, case now cradled in his arms. Thompson wasn't sure if it actually was the flutter of pigeons vying for the best roosts. It seemed louder than that. More substantial. It came again.

'I asked you,' Crowther moaned, nostrils flaring in and out. 'I asked you and you said there was no other way in here. Has it got a door?'

Thompson glanced over his shoulder. This was...this was totally absurd. 'No.'

'No? What's there, then?'

'Nothing. It's an open archway, that's all.'

Crowther let out a whimper. He reached into the case and brought the cellophane package out. 'Take it! You take it!'

Thompson stepped back, lifting his hands in protest. 'I don't – '

'Take it!' Crowther shrieked. 'You're a priest. Take it!'

Thompson thought, you're right. I am a priest. And this is my church. He turned his palms up. 'Whatever this is – '

But Crowther was past him, running for the door that led out into the churchyard. Case in one hand, he fumbled at the key with his other, whining like a child. The noise on the stairs was definitely getting louder. It sounded like light footsteps: someone coming down the steep flight of stone steps at speed. The skin of Thompson's scalp drew tight.

Crowther was now tugging desperately at the door. 'Open! Open! Why won't you – '

'The bolt,' Thompson pointed out, still trying to understand what was happening.

Crowther's hand shot up. He yanked it across then

barged the door open with his shoulder. Before Thompson could say anything more, the other man had fled into the night.

The priest looked at the dark pathway, the sound of Crowther's footsteps rapidly dying. The ones descending the tower were getting closer. Thompson drew in a deep breath. 'Hello?' His voice wavered. He sounded scared. 'Who is that?'

The rhythm of the footsteps didn't change. He stared at the motionless wall-hanging. How many steps did the tower have? One hundred and twelve. He counted fourteen footsteps in a matter of seconds. The person was flying down at breakneck speed. 'Mrs Reynolds? Who is that, please?'

Another four steps. And another. A few seconds more and the person would be at the bottom. The door leading out to the graveyard was swinging shut. The gap was narrowing. A voice was yelling in his head. He realised it had been yelling for some time. Get out! Get out! Get out!

CHAPTER 28

Cool night air hit him. Above him, faint clumps of orange-washed cloud looked superimposed on the dark sky. Crowther had vanished in the direction of the main road. A single-deck bus was trundling by. Its bright windows framed the massed passengers within. Lined in neat rows, each of their heads was bowed as if in deep contemplation. Eyes on screens, headphones clamping ears. All of them shut off in their separate worlds. He could shout, but no one would hear.

Is this really happening, he thought, slamming the door shut.

He took one stride towards the presbytery where he lived on the far side of the graveyard, then changed his mind. Turning back to the door, he opened it a few inches. The footsteps now sounded so close, he thought the wall-hanging was about to be swept aside. Willing his hand to stop shaking, he reached through the gap for the key. His thumb and forefinger found it just as the footsteps came to a halt. From the corner of his eye, he saw the heavy material begin to bulge. Thompson tugged at the key: it wouldn't come out. Whatever was pressing against the wall-hanging started moving to the side. As the key finally came free, Thompson thought he saw white fingers curling round the edge of the material.

He pushed the door shut and inserted the key. He didn't know why, but locking the door from the outside was always far more difficult. Something – rust? – meant it only ever turned stiffly and slowly. The footsteps started again, in the vestry now. Twisting the key with all his might, he managed a three-quarter rotation and felt the thing engage a moment before the footsteps came to a halt on the other side of the door. The metal latch lifted rapidly up and down, a mad telegraph message into the night.

'Who is that?' Thompson demanded. 'Who is there?'

Silence.

'It's locked. And so are the main doors at the front. Until you speak, they remain that way.'

No answer.

He brought an ear close to the wood and listened. The person on the other side made no sound. Not even breathing. How could they not be out of breath after all that running? Thompson considered whether to take the key out and peep through the key hole. No, he decided. I'm going to call the police, tell them I've locked an intruder inside the church. He turned his back on the building and started across the graveyard.

After the fork, the right-hand path followed a lazy S ending at the presbytery. Half-jogging, half-walking, he felt his breath becoming more and more ragged. The ache in his lungs as spreading. A thin pain kept extended into his left shoulder with every thud of his heart. Twenty or so metres from his front door, he realised he had to stop. If I don't, he told himself, I might keel over.

He slowed to a walk and decided to the check the church. Apart from the single glowing window of the vestry toilet, the entire building was black and lifeless. Did it happen? He raised a hand and patted a bulging lump of white hair back in place. Being clear of the building allowed him to think. He'd heard of cases where hysteria jumped from one person to another, like an infection. Entire crowds became convinced of the most impossible things.

Crowther's story was churning in his head. The man

had held him – trapped as a captive audience – for well over an hour. First on the church pews, then in the vestry. The two of them, facing each other across the small table. In that time, the story had gradually spread its tentacles, enmeshed him, bound him up.

He looked again at the lit window of the vestry toilet. He thought about how Crowther had nipped in there. Had he got another phone on him? Did he call Sullivan from behind the toilet's closed door and tell him to ring the phone he'd conveniently left on the table in the vestry?

The church was obviously deserted. Thompson looked around, as if waking from a dream. The noise of the road, the familiar tombstones, the Yew tree standing by the corner of the church. His eyes lifted to the squat tower. The spire had never been built and its square shape gave it a castle-like appearance. The ornate window frames at the top contained no glass and the flimsy mesh always came loose. That's how pigeons got in. The largest of the windows was circular. Emerging from it, pale limbs like those of a monstrous spider, was a person.

Thompson span round and started running for his house.

CHAPTER 29

Barely able to breath, he reached the steps up to the door and forced himself up them. Pressing a hand against wood, he tried to suck in air, eyes closed, as he delved in his trouser pocket for his keys. Dragging them out, he looked back. The figure was now on the ledge that ran beneath the church's upper tier of windows. Sideways steps – nimble and fast – took it to the corner of the building. Thompson watched with terrified fascination as it leapt the small space into the top of the Yew tree.

It disappeared into the foliage and Thompson got his door open, stepped inside and slammed it shut. He swiped his hand across a panel of brass light switches then put his hands on his knees, fighting the urge to just drop to the tiled floor and curl up. Head hanging forwards, he tried to make sense of what was going on. Part of him was outraged and incredulous. This wasn't possible. It couldn't be. But that voice was small and insignificant when compared to the primal chorus that clamoured and bellowed and roared of the danger he was in.

He realised his left hand still held the package containing Maggy Wallace's hair. A reflex reaction sent it flying away from him. It span across the hard surface and came to a halt against the skirting board. Was the back door bolted? Yes. Always locked since the attempted break-in earlier in the year. Same as the side doors out to the patio. Windows? He ran a mental check: he hadn't opened a ground floor one in months. First floor? The insurance company had insisted on little square locks being fitted to all of them. The house was secure.

A noise came from outside. It was here, he realised. Outside on the pathway. Soon it would be mounting the front steps. I must call the police. Now.

He stepped toward the small table at the base of the stairs. Beside a foot high statue of a pilgrim holding a staff was the telephone. Then the cellophane package caught his eye. Inside it, long white tresses stretched from one end to the other. Changing direction, he lumbered over to the package, dropped to one knee, scooped it up and turned his head to the door.

A wavery figure was gradually taking shape beyond the frosted glass. He struggled back to his feet. 'Here! Have it back. I never wanted it.'

It approached slowly.

'Do you understand? Please, I swear to God, I'm not part of this. It belongs to you.'

He edged closer to the door. The letter box was just below the window panel. He could see the figure more clearly now, the shape of its bare skull, the shadowy eye sockets. Had it heard him? Was it waiting?

Thompson lifted the copper flap of the letter box up. Only as he started to feed the end of the package through the opening, did he realise it felt too light. He glanced down. Most of the contents were missing. As it was yanked violently from his fingers, he saw the bottom end had come apart. He looked back and heard his own anguished cry. Long white strands formed a delicate trail across the hallway, right to his feet.

The sound of movement outside. He turned. The figure was climbing up the side of the porch. The roof, he realised. The attic room only he ever entered.

Inside it was a single window.

It was set into the sloping ceiling and opened out on a hinge at its midpoint.

Because heat rose up the central staircase to the top of the house, he always left it partly open. Otherwise, the room grew unbearably stuffy. He knew the door into the room would be locked. But that didn't matter. He let out a groan of despair. The lock he'd fitted to it could be released from the inside.

By the first landing, Thompson's throat felt like boiling water had been poured down it. Grimacing with pain, he glanced up. The central staircase let him see all the way to the attic, unbroken banister turning back on itself. Three more flights.

Come on, he demanded, slapping at his legs. Work, you bastards.

He made the first floor and kept going. Two more flights. Extending his left hand, he clamped it on the banister and dragged himself higher. He realised he was grunting with each step. He tried to use it as a rhythm. Up. Up. Up. Stepping round the last landing, he tried to assess the final climb. But his vision was clouding. The pain in his left shoulder now jabbed down into his forearm.

It's not much further, he told himself. Not much.

Keeping his left hand on the banister, he lifted his right foot onto the first step. With his free hand, he pushed down on his raised knee. One by one, he made his way laboriously to the top. Wheezing and coughing, he rummaged in his pocket and brought out his keys. The Yale lock was bronze and the key that fitted it shorter than the others. He got it in the lock and pushed the door open.

CHAPTER 30

The room was long and narrow. Its walls extended up to a height of about five feet before sloping inwards. The space seemed smaller than it really was because of the images that coated every surface. Their borders pressed up against each other; a solid bank of pictures vying for attention. Mandy Cost on a photo shoot, modelling underwear. Mandy Cost on a beach, wearing a miniscule bikini. Mandy Cost emerging from a gym in Lycra leggings and a crop top. Mandy Cost on the way into a nightclub, breasts barely within a low-cut top. Mandy Cost swinging her legs out of a taxi, a triangle of white cotton just visible below the hem of her micro dress. In some of the photos, her hair was the palest platinum: what now lay strewn across his hallway floor.

The single window was built into the angled section of ceiling at the room's far end. To his right was a printer and scanner – one capable of producing the A3 size images coating the walls. Beside it was a stack of spare ink cartridges and a rack of magazines, from which some of the photos had been sourced. But the majority of his collection came from the internet.

To his left was the computer, hooked up to the biggest monitor he could find. After the ladies in the church had told him who Mandy Cost was, he'd made his first tentative search on the church-provided computer downstairs. He couldn't believe how many pictures of her existed. Scrolling through them, he soon came across shots that were more revealing.

He didn't click on any during that first visit. But they wouldn't leave his head: his mind had been branded. Making his breakfast, reading his books, planning his sermons, her image was always hovering.

When she'd next returned, clunking up the aisle in her heels, his throat had grown tight. It was to keep control, he told himself. That's why he'd separated her persona from her person. The media version of Mandy Cost was wanton and lewd, available and willing. The stuff of fantasy. But it wasn't actually her. He knew that. So it was OK, he'd said to himself, buying the second computer. As long as he kept the artificial version of her distinct from the actual young woman who came to his church.

And it had worked, for a while. Up here, during his lonely evenings, he'd studied and scrutinised her. He soon found the site selling the ex-lover's home-made video.

That had caused him close to three weeks' dilemma. He knew watching it would be unforgivable. He also knew it would cross a mental line he'd set. Intimate images of her, in bed with her lover. He'd tried to resist, but it was useless.

And he was right: after watching it, things did change. Now, when she talked to him – so vulnerable, so exposed – his mind replayed those images from her bed. As she whispered to him, he tried not to look at her lips. But he couldn't stop himself. So, when only the two of them were in the church, he'd suggested using a confessional booth. With a partition between them, he just had her voice. Within a month, he'd started recording her words, holding the little device just below the latticed screen.

He worked out how to transfer the audio files to his computer. He edited out his own murmured questions so it was just her statements. He'd listen to them late into the night as he pored over his collection of images.

A bumping scrape brought him back to the present. The

window! He had to get the window shut. The noise came again. It was above and just behind him. She had made it to the roof, was climbing on to the tiles. From there, it wasn't far to the apex of the large house. When she reached that, the window on the far side would be visible.

He started forward again, heavy feet thudding on the wooden floor boards. The noise – now just behind his head – seemed to keep track. He had to get there first, grab the handle, pull it down and flick the lock at its base. He tried to speed up but, halfway across the room, something prevented his left foot from swinging forward. To his side, the printer suddenly rotated then slid outwards. Both he and the machine started falling. The wire, he thought. The wire connecting it to the computer.

As he pitched forwards, he got his hands up, but the impact with the attic floor was still a shock. Both knees connected with the wooden boards, swiftly followed by his elbows, right hip and head. The printer and a load of cartridges crashed down beside him.

He blinked. The rough wood pressing against his face wouldn't come into focus. Get up, he urged, lifting himself to his elbows. You must get up! As he craned his head back to check the window, Maggy Wallace dropped silently into the room.

CHAPTER 31

Father Ian Thompson recoiled across the floor, limbs scrabbling for purchase.

On landing, she had sunk into a deep squatting position, one hand resting on the floorboards, head bowed. Her long dress was blackened and dirty. Her scalp looked raw and painful. Clumps of scorched hair remained, stray wisps standing from the sides of her head. He was reminded of 1940s photos when France had been liberated: female collaborators had been dragged from their homes by baying mobs. Slapped and spat at, their hair had been roughly shorn and they'd been shoved forwards through the streets, weeping with distress and shame.

The woman before him wasn't weeping. The woman before him was motionless. Thompson kept shuffling quietly backward, trying to increase the space between them. What had happened to her? Perhaps the demonic force that drove her had been exhausted. Another few feet, he thought, and I'll be in the doorway. If I can get through it and slam the door shut, it might take her a few seconds to open it again. Getting down the stairs won't take me long. He could picture the main path straight back to the road. Streetlights. Cars. Normality.

He slid himself back another few inches and the floorboard beneath him creaked. Slowly, her head started to lift. Thompson didn't want to see her face. He knew it would be terrible.

But he couldn't take his eyes off her.

Large sections of skin were charred and blistered. The bits that weren't seemed drained of blood. Grey. Without life. Her cold eyes didn't blink. Instead, they stared straight ahead, focused on nothing. He wondered for a second if she was blind. If the flames had blinded her. But she had been dead when they'd taken hold. How could this be happening! He waited, but she was like a statue. Maybe she wasn't interested in him after all. Perhaps she thought she had been following Crowther. As he eased himself back once again, the keys in his pocket chinked.

Her eyes shifted a fraction and, before he could prevent it, their gazes met.

Instantly, her pupils shrank. He felt the terrible pull of those twin dots and tried to wrench his eyes away. But their blackness was beyond him. It was a blackness that swamped all sound, stretched out time, sucked at his breath. Her lips parted, teeth clenched tight as her body began to rear up.

Utter terror engulfed him. He half-turned, one hand pushing against the floor. He found himself on his feet, stumbling. She was now behind him and he could feel the malevolence of her stare on his back. His spine writhed. The doorway was in reaching distance. Beyond it was the top step, banister sloping down. As he stretched out a hand, he heard a single footstep, then another. Bony fingers suddenly clamped on his shoulders and started carrying him forward.

The realisation of how Mandy Cost died was suddenly clear. He tensed, trying to bend his legs, twisting his body and flailing for the doorframe with his right hand. But it was already too far behind him. Forced on by her, he brought his left arm out in an attempt to grasp the banister. But she was so strong. His fingers wrapped round the smooth length of wood but his momentum was too much. The banister connected with his hips and his upper body immediately started to fold over it. The yawning stairwell opened up below him. Then his feet lifted from the floor, his legs came up and he was over, dropping face first towards the tiled floor of the hallway thirty feet below.

CHRIS SIMMS

CHAPTER 32

Nigel Crowther kept his eyes closed and listened. The rapid pattering sound that had woken him continued. It had a steady, unchanging cadence that was quite pleasant. It meant only one thing: rain. Not heavy – the water he could hear coming down the drainpipe of his little cabin was more of a trickle than a torrent. He imagined a fine drizzle that drifted, rather than dropped. A common occurrence along this stretch of the Norfolk coast.

He opened his eyes to darkness. How long, he wondered, has it been since I've woken to such peace? No sirens, beeps or alarms. No shouting or roller bins rumbling. Bottles clattering. The unceasing intrusion of streetlight. The temporary blue flash of emergency vehicles speeding by. City life.

He realised it had been almost two years since his previous stay. Just after the time Joe Sullivan had rented it from him. In the twenty or so months since, he'd been boxed in by concrete, glass and steel. It had been too long.

He'd arrived in the early hours, mentally exhausted from almost two days spent driving around England's motorway network. The darkness had been absolute and, after parking as close to the front door as possible, he'd relied on the tiny LED torch in the fob of his car keys to find the front door's lock. Post was piled thick inside the door. The usual assortment of promotional junk. He'd swept it all up and left it on the side in the kitchen. A job for the next day.

Crowther looked to his left: his phone was beside the bed. The screen came to life as he touched the side button. Six-forty-seven a.m. It would start getting light soon. The process of getting out of London had been nerve-wracking, especially when traffic had almost slowed to a halt near Heathrow on the M25. He'd peered nervously about, thankful for the presence of so many other people. Their proximity both reassured him and sharpened his sense of isolation. None of them could help him. None of them would even believe him. All he could do was keep moving.

He'd driven up the M1 as far as Leeds, before booking into a motel once he was too tired to go any further. After getting a few hours of fitful sleep, he'd taken to the road once again, this time driving west, then south, unsure where he was heading. Over the course of the morning, his mind continued to race, repeatedly going over everything that had happened. Gradually, he'd formed a theory. One that, the more he analysed it, the better it seemed to work.

Trees.

Apart from Maggy Wallace's hair, there was another link between everyone who'd died. Each person had been in the proximity of a tree when she'd struck.

While Mandy Cost had been jogging, she'd seen Wallace among the branches of one in the local park. Shortly after, she'd jumped through the second floor window of a house with a huge tree growing right outside it. Before committing suicide, Gregory Lang had seen her in the trees beside the mental health unit. Joe Sullivan's phone message: he'd spotted Maggy Wallace up in an oak tree. Even the kids she'd chosen to help – the youngest one said she'd descended from the canopy above them. The woman had loved to climb trees. She'd lived in a bloody forest.

As he'd escaped from Father Thompson's church, Crowther had noticed the large Yew tree which stood at the corner of the building. It made sense: she'd climbed up it and got into the church through the tower windows at the top. That's how she struck: from on high.

The realisation was concrete. It was the first relief he'd felt in days. Suddenly, he knew exactly where he needed to go. Approaching the next motorway junction, he realised he was near Bath. He needed to go east. East towards his little beachside retreat on the secluded stretch of coast.

As he drove, his mind kept flicking to the priest. Mandy Cost had said to Joe Sullivan that the old boy wasn't quite right. When she'd first visited the church, he'd been so kind and understanding. But his attitude had gradually shifted. He'd started wanting to know more and more about the men she spent time with. How long it took before she slept with each one. Where the act took place. If she'd been drinking or using drugs. She'd guessed that – even though he was a priest – he didn't need to know those things. So she'd decided to switch to a different church: one run by a female vicar.

Crowther thought about the book he and Sullivan had been planning. The section on Mandy's strange need to discuss her existence with an old priest was never going to be a major part of it. The audience it was intended for wouldn't have been interested. They'd want the celebrity scandals, they disgruntled ex-boyfriends, the bitter wives who blamed Mandy for their broken marriages. A photo of a church and speculation about whether she was searching for the father she'd never had wasn't going to shift many copies. Crowther couldn't understand why the priest had got so defensive every time he'd mentioned her visits to the church. Unless Joe's theory had been correct: the old man was secretly turned on by her.

Crowther sat up in bed. He wanted to check the internet – the previous day, he could find nothing about a priest being found dead. Now it was almost ten hours later. A long time in the news cycle. He grabbed his phone and peeled the duvet back. Cold. Always was when he hadn't visited for a while. He put on a dressing gown and slippers, and went through to the kitchen. Later that day, he'd get the stove lit. But, for now, he'd have to use the fan heater to warm the room up. As the machine whirred to life, he took the laptop out of his leather attaché case. After turning the machine on, he stared absent-mindedly out the window. A faint smear of gold was showing on the eastern horizon. Soon it would be light enough to see and hear the rain. On the floor inside the door were the two boxes of food he'd bought at the supermarket in Caister-on-Sea. Enough to last a few weeks, especially if he hooked the odd fish from the sea.

If he needed to, he'd stay here permanently. As he'd followed the country lanes, he'd thought of his little cabin as something that could save his life. The reason for that was very simple: there were absolutely no trees in the vicinity. Apart from a few low shrubs, the entire stretch of coast was devoid of them. The cabin lay on the edge of countryside that was – to some – depressingly flat; acres of sugar beet fields, a narrow swathe of beach and then endless miles of sea. Nothing that towered over the cabin. In fact, nothing tall within sight.

Outside, the rainwater continued on its noisy way down the drain. Mixing with it, he thought he heard another noise, almost like a sizzle or a buzz. He tried to sift it from the other sounds, wondering for a moment if it was the fan heater going wrong. But the machine seemed to be working fine.

As the laptop gradually came to life, he flicked through the post. Nothing interesting. A few envelopes carried the crest of the local council alongside the logo of Mistral energy, the French outfit that had been awarded the contract to build the controversial wind farm further along the coast.

The laptop had now found a mobile phone signal strong enough to give him access to the internet. He logged on and immediately checked the same news service feeds he always favoured. Within a couple of minutes, a report caused his finger to lift from the scroll button. It was about the tragic death of an elderly priest who, it appeared, had lost his balance and fallen over an upstairs banister in his house.

The body of Father Ian Thompson had been seen the previous day by the church cleaner, a Mrs Rosemary Reynolds, when she'd peeped through the letterbox trying to work out why the priest hadn't opened up the church.

Crowther sat back, one finger tapping against the laptop's casing. Fallen over the banister from an upstairs floor of his house. He knew it was no accident: she'd got him. Crowther let out a long shuddering sigh. He hadn't planned to force Maggy Wallace's hair onto the priest. He'd wanted to discuss it with him, ask him to take it. He coughed guiltily. He may as well have shoved the priest into the path of a speeding tube train. I killed him, he said to himself. To save my own life, I killed him. No, he thought. That's not true; you didn't plan to leave him with the hair. At least, not the way it worked out. The church tower's steps, they changed everything.

He read through the newswire story again. Thompson had been found in his house, not the church. He must have got out, made it across to the presbytery. But she'd followed him. And there could be only one explanation for that: the hair. Thompson had been in possession of all of it – every single strand. Surely she'd got it back. She had what she'd wanted so very badly.

He looked at the window and, for the first time, dared hope he had survived the ordeal. The base of the sky was now a dirty yellow. He could see rain droplets clinging to the window. The day was about to begin. The room felt hot, so he reached over to the fan heater and switched it off.

The electric whoosh slowly lost strength, but the faint crackling continued. He frowned. Some kind of ship, maybe? Or one of those motorised paragliders? Except it was dark. Who flew about in the dark? He flicked the switch of the kettle and turned to the window once more. Levels of light were now just strong enough to see outside. The beach was shrouded in a pale mist; the kind that never survived long in the light of day. A couple of clouds were visible in the lower sky and the drizzle was easing off.

He lined up a cup and spoon alongside the kettle. After a minute, it turned itself off. The bubbling water settled and he could make out the noise again. A faint metallic buzz, like a swarm of a million robot bees. What the hell was it?

He decided to ring the front desk of *Snapped!* and get someone to make a call or two. Find out more details about the priest's death. Crowther suspected there would be details that had the police puzzled. While they were doing that, a few enquiries about Joe Sullivan would be useful, too. He picked his phone off the table. Almost out of battery. Damn it. The charger was in the attaché case. He reached inside and sought out the lead he'd shoved in there while swiftly packing a few things after fleeing the church.

The noise registered again. A buzz, but with small pops, too. He checked the window. Now he could clearly see the beach and first thirty metres or so of sea. The water was grey and calm. No sign of anything moored nearby. Odd.

He lifted the charger out, placed it on the table and reached for his phone. As he did so, something gossamer-like tightened across the skin of his knuckles. He looked down but could see nothing. Raising his fingers up, he was just able to make out a mass of fine wisps trailing in the air. Hair. Filaments of long silver hair.

He stood, heart suddenly pumping. He felt lightheaded. Some must have slipped out of the cellophane wrapper while it had been in his attaché. He felt ill as he shook his hand back and forth. But the strands had wrapped themselves round his fingers too well. The sink, he thought. The quickest way to get them off me.

But then they'd be down the plug-hole, lying in the pipes. He didn't want them anywhere near his home. The sea, then. He'd sluice his hand about in the shallows, let the ocean carry them away.

He unbolted the door, pulled it open and stepped out. The air felt clammy. Droplets hung from the underside of the guttering. As he trudged quickly down the gentle bank of coarse grass onto the pebbly beach, he realised the weird noise was louder. A persistent hissing. It seemed to be drifting down from the sky above him. He stopped and looked left along the deserted beach.

Its gentle curve ended at a low headland about six hundred metres away. Half-shrouded by mist on its furthest point was a structure both insect-like and alien. Six horizontal arms stood out from the upper part of a central section. Forty or fifty metres high, the weak sun was enmeshed in its precisely arranged struts. Each branch-like arm ended in a downward pointing finger. From each of these there stretched a cable. The cables, sagging slightly, ran to an identical structure, this one slightly back from the beach and a couple of hundred metres closer. The cables from this one continued towards Crowther. His eyes followed the metallic strands to a third structure, this one less than two hundred metres away.

Turning his head in the other direction, he looked off to his right. The pylons continued, a column of them marching inland. He remembered the local protests about the offshore wind farm. It didn't bother him: he wasn't here much and the turbines weren't going to be visible from his cabin. So he'd only skimmed over the subsequent letters about the proposed route the pylons would take to transport the electricity to the nearest substation.

With a feeling of trepidation, he looked to his left once more. The cables looped on towards his property. He turned fully round. Like tree trunks, the pylon's four feet were firmly planted in the field directly to the side of his cabin. He forced his eyes up the looming tower, past the highly-charged cables that hissed and fizzed in the moist air, past the uppermost pair of arms to the very top.

Perched there was a figure, the hem of its skirt hanging down.

From the angle of its bald head, Crowther knew it was looking straight at him. A breeze stirred the strands of hair entwining his fingers and the figure's head tilted. Crowther whirled round and fled towards the slate-coloured sea.

The instant he splashed into the shallows, his slippers flooded with ice cold water. He kept going up to his knees, then came to a stop, tearful eyes fixed on the far horizon. 'Oh, Lord, forgive me, please forgive me, I beg your forgiveness. I want to serve you, I'll be your servant, I open myself to you and your power.' He scooped seawater up in his palm and tipped it over his bowed head. 'Yours is the power and the glory.' He repeated the action, liquid running down his face and neck and into his pyjama top. 'I ask for your blessing and for your protection. Make her go away, please, Lord.'

With a sharp intake of breath, he looked over his shoulder.

The figure was now at the lowermost horizontal strut. Crowther brushed the water from his eyes, desperate to clear his vision. She was no longer there. He didn't dare breathe. A second or two passed. Had she gone? Swallowed by the air itself?

She straightened up from the long grass at the base of the pylon. Seawater stung his eyes and he had to blink heavily. Now she was on the shingle, racing towards him, skirt flapping about her spindly legs.

Moaning in terror, Crowther started wading rapidly into deeper water. The gravelly bottom fell away and suddenly he was up to his neck. The sea was freezing. Gasping with shock, he tried to back pedal, but his leg slipped, then buckled. Briny liquid closed over his face and he flailed his arms about. He broke through the surface.

The ocean enveloping him was so brutally cold his bones felt like they were shrinking. Trying to tread water, dressing gown heavy on his shoulders, he looked back to the beach.

She was at the water's edge.

He watched her for a good minute, but she didn't move. 'Wha...' the word was sucked back into his mouth as a spasm shook him. 'What do you want? Please, I did...I ... I...' his lips were so numb, he couldn't control his speech, '...I didn't mean for...this. Pl-please!'

She stood motionless, shadow pooled in her eye sockets.

Kicking weakly with his legs, Crowther looked off to his left and right. Flat sea, empty sand. Only able to swim doggy-paddle, he started towards the distant headland, hoping someone might be on the next beach. Every time he looked to the beach, she was opposite him. After a minute he could go no further and stopped. He lifted his face to the sky and tried to bellow for help, but nothing would come out. The cold was making him pant. Glancing back towards land, he realised he was further out to sea. He was drifting.

Strands of sodden hair started to obscure his vision and he lifted a hand from the water to sweep it from his face. A thumb connected with his nose. He tried again but his hand was shaking so badly, he hit himself in the temple. He realised he could no longer flex his fingers. All sensation was gone from his legs. He tried to beat his arms faster, but they wouldn't respond. A sense of sleepiness was trickling into his mind. Only when he breathed water in through his nose did he realise he was sinking. Coughing and blinking, he thrashed with the last of his strength. The ocean was turning to syrup, sucking away his will. Moving was so hard. Easier to not bother; it didn't feel so cold now, after all. Yes, it wasn't so cold. Not too cold at all. He felt water seeping into his mouth and nostrils once more, and just before he slipped beneath the

surface, he looked towards the beach.
She was a sentinel, silent and still.

EPILOGUE

Page 9, *The Norwich Mercury.*

A body, clothed only in pyjamas, and washed ashore six days ago on a remote Norfolk beach, has been identified as that of Nigel Crowther, forty-seven-years-old, a picture editor at the popular weekly magazine, Snapped!

Reported as missing by his employer last Monday, Mr Crowther was unmarried and lived in London, but owned a beachside bungalow less than five miles from the spot where his body was found.

The original Norfolk police appeal for information, issued when the body was first discovered, described a male of average height and build with white hair.

Police are not looking for anyone else in connection to his death.

THE END

ACKNOWLEDGEMENTS

All my thanks to Jim K for his excellent suggestions at improving the plot.

Praise for *Chris Simms* –

'I'll be downloading more of Chris Simms' books ASAP. I feel like I've discovered a hidden gem.' (*Amazon Reader review*)

'Chris Simms has never shown any reluctance to chill the blood of the reader.' *(GOOD BOOK GUIDE)*

'Simms has written a gritty novel that grips from start to finish. I just couldn't put it down.' (*HORRORSCOPE*)

'After many years of reviewing... it's not often my jaded nerves get actually, physically jangled.' (*MORNING STAR*)

'A chilling thriller, this will have you leaving the light on when you climb into bed.' (*LOVE READING*)

About the Author

Chris Simms' acclaimed first novel in the DI Spicer series, *Killing The Beasts* was selected as a Best Crime Book for 2005 by Shots magazine. He was then selected as a *Waterstone's Author for the Future*, one of 25 writers tipped by publishers, editors and agents, to produce the most impressive body of work over the next quarter century. Since then he has been nominated several times for the *Theakston's Crime Novel of the Year* and for *Crime Writers' Association Daggers*. Chris lives near Manchester.

Discover more at: www.chrissimms.info

SING ME TO SLEEP

A Supernatural Thriller

Laura and Owen's new home should be lovely. But soon after moving into the secluded cottage on the edge of the Peak District, Laura starts to hear faint snatches of birdsong.

Her husband, wrapped up in his job, is rarely at home. Nervous and confused, Laura cannot decide whether the noise is real – or if it's coming from inside her head. Her doctor can find nothing wrong with her hearing. Then an archaeological dig on a neighbouring hill unearths some disturbing finds – and Laura's life starts to become terrifying...

PROLOGUE

The men stared at the hole in grim silence.

She turned away from the hushed group to gaze across the dull field at a finger of bright snow. It clung stubbornly to life in the shadow of a dry stone wall. She realised, wrapping her shawl more tightly about herself, it was the last visible evidence of the brutal storm from a fortnight before.

From below their feet a disembodied voice called out. 'OK, carry on!'

The fire fighter holding the winch started turning it once more, winding in a length of rope that dropped like a plumb-line into the dark cleft.

The heads of his colleagues stayed bowed, as did those of three policemen, a man in an overcoat and a vicar. A funeral, she thought. It looks just like a funeral. But no body was being buried. The reverse, in fact.

A yellowish glow broke the blackness at their feet. She looked on impassively as the dirt-smeared head and shoulders of a man rose slowly out of the ground. In the harsh light of day, the lamp on his miner's helmet was suddenly useless. His arms came into view. They were cradling something loosely wrapped in blue plastic sheeting.

She knew exactly what it was.

The man had now been winched high enough to get a

knee on the brick-lined rim. He held the bundle out. Reluctantly, a policeman took it. Without looking at it properly, he laid it on the wiry turf and backed away.

All eyes went to the man in the overcoat. After sending an uncomfortable glance in the lone woman's direction, he crouched down and tentatively lifted the corner. A collective jolt passed through the group and the vicar's legs suddenly folded. He sat down in the long cold grass and started to claw at his dog collar, only stopping when his shirt was torn open. Moaning weakly, he turned in the woman's direction.

But she was already striding away, shawl now pulled over her head. A veil.

CHAPTER 1

He crossed his legs and the folds in his corduroys reminded her of the undulating land surrounding her new home. 'So, tell me about this…dream of yours.'

She hesitated before replying. Was it his tone? He just didn't feel very doctorly. From somewhere outside his surgery came the shrill sound of a startled bird. She glanced nervously at the frosted glass before looking back at the doctor. Bushy brows formed an unbroken crest above his narrowed eyes. She felt pinned by his unblinking stare.

The window behind him glowed with late autumnal sunlight. It caught on the thick hairs protruding from his ears. Like antennae, hanging there in space. Antennae not very well attuned to more delicate thoughts and feelings, she suspected.

Her right hand lifted and fingers moved slightly as she began to speak. 'It feels so similar to the one I used to have.'

He reached for her medical notes, causing her words to falter and stop. She thought: he surely read the top sheet before I opened his door. Any good doctor did that. So he knew the basics. The surface detail. Laura Wilkinson, thirty-nine years old, five feet eight, excellent physical health, no allergies, blood type O, a shade over nine stone.

As she'd first stepped inside, he'd half-risen from his chair, directing her to the empty seat beside his desk with a flash of palm. His eyes touched her face in a cursory sort of way. Then they'd returned for another look.

She'd often been told she was attractive – though why people said that she never could fathom. She liked her hair. Long and pale and windblown when she let it hang loose. Combing it and arranging it had always given her so much pleasure – always, ever since she was very young. But she was convinced there was too much of a gap between her eyes and she found the bones of her face harsh. When she closed her lips, she could see the swell of her teeth behind them.

Her husband, Owen, had assured her many times that her bone structure was beautiful. Sometimes, she just sensed her skull when she looked in the mirror. Lurking there. Waiting, one day, to show itself.

'Carry on, I'm listening,' he prompted, leafing back through the pages. There were lots.

'It feels so similar,' she tentatively repeated. But eye contact had gone, and with it the feeling he was taking her words in. She persevered. 'A tunnel. Narrow, dark, cold. Horribly cold. The same sense of abandonment, of needing warmth and comfort - but being so alone. This time though, the child – it's too indistinct to tell if it's male or female – isn't lying at the end of the tunnel. And it's not curled in a foetal position, either. It's nearer - '

'This previous dream. The one from six years ago?'

'Yes.' His head was still down as he studied the pages. She could see her previous doctor's hand-written additions. The elegant, neat letters somehow conveyed how kind she was. Dr Ford added something in a harsh scrawl.

'The time when you and Owen were trying to start a family?'

'Yes.'

'And you began to feel anxious and unhappy when that proved unproductive?'

There it was again. Unproductive. How tactless of him,

she thought, considering whether to lean forward and yank one of the monstrous hairs from his ears. She wondered if he'd yelp. 'That was all prior to the series of fertility tests I underwent.'

He looked up with a questioning expression.

'There was nothing wrong with me, you see. That wasn't the problem. Which means – you know – that the reason I couldn't conceive...that was down to Owen. His sperm count.' Introducing Owen into the equation seemed to unsettle the doctor slightly, judging from the way he shifted in his seat. He looked down at her notes once more.

Twenty-three years, she thought. The age difference between Owen and I. It had seemed so utterly irrelevant when they'd first met. Back then, the attention of an older man – and one widely tipped for greatness – had, if anything, been a thrill. Her mother had her reservations. Gentle hints about the long-term which Laura – made giddy with love - had blithely swept aside

Her eyes drifted to the bright pictures on the wall above his examination bed. Images from fairytales, placed there to make younger patients feel more comfortable. Her favourite was right in the middle. Snow White. Rabbits gambolled at her feet and birds fluttered about her head. Before the witch appeared and ruined everything.

'And when you made the decision not to have children, the dream faded away of its own accord?' Doctor Ford asked.

Faded? Of its own accord? It was obliterated, she wanted to yell. By the drugs they pumped into me. And we didn't make the decision not to have children. Owen decided for both of us when he refused to undergo any tests. 'I went to see a dream therapist. My previous doctor - Helen Evans – she put me in touch with him.'

He sat back. 'A dream therapist?'

'Yes.' She wondered if it was his accent that made him seem so...unfeeling. The northern gruffness.

'Down in London was this?'

She nodded. 'He said the image of the curled-up child – its position in a cold, dark passage – that was my mind trying to represent not being able to get pregnant. The passage was my womb, the lack of warmth my perceived infertility - '

'Well, I'd prefer not to conjecture on the symbolism of dreams. If you feel that you need to be referred for some counselling, I'm sure - '

'No.' The word came out with too much force. 'Sorry. No. I feel fine. Happy. The whole thing about having babies doesn't bother me anymore. I mean, I'm thirty-nine. It would be silly.'

'But this dream bothers you?'

Her fingers started to flutter once more. She saw his eyes intently tracking their movement. The psychiatrists used to do that, too. She placed her hand back in her lap. 'Yes. It's similar, not the same. The figure – I'll call it a him because I sense its male – is much nearer to...to what I can tell is the opening. The way out into the world. But his position is all awkward; the knees are apart, an elbow is jutting out. One hand is bent back behind the head. Like he's jammed. He can't move. It's a horrible image.'

She heard the thin whistle of air passing up his nostrils. It must, she thought, be hairy up there, too. 'Have you discussed this with your husband?'

She shook her head. 'No – the dream has only started recently. The last month. Since we moved into Lantern Cottage. I'm not sure if it isn't related to the funny noise that I've been - ' His eyebrows twitched and, for the briefest instant, she spotted something in his eyes.

'What noise?'

'It's like a bird singing. It comes and goes. Owen hasn't heard it yet. But I have. It's not unpleasant – it's too beautiful for that. But it's started to frustrate me.' She paused. 'No, the fact I can't figure out where it's coming from has started to frustrate me. It seems to float.' His eyes were moving about and she realised they were following her fingers. She thought: I'm motioning again. Reaching for thistledown, as Owen calls it. 'It's always too indistinct to pinpoint. I can't tell if it's in the house or not.' She glanced at his computer terminal. 'I had a look on the internet.' She laughed nervously. 'You don't think it could be tinnitus, do you?'